Summer trade at Keith Calder's gunshop in the Square at Newton Lauder is slack, so when he interviews a candidate for a job his questions are more searching than they might otherwise have been. The prospective employee, Robert Hall, seems very well suited for the job, but his refusal to allow Keith to take up references is worrying. So Keith presses Hall for more details, and the tale he is told concerning Hall's former employer contains some damning and sinister allegations.

From snatches of overheard conversation Hall gathered that his boss was working on a gun conversion. Usual enough, except that the alterations being made and the secrecy surrounding the work added up to only one thing – an assassination weapon.

Naturally Keith Calder suggests going to the police, and when the call is put through to the local station it quickly reaches the desk of Sergeant Ian Fellowes, Keith's prospective son-in-law and local Firearms Officer. As police investigations progress, Ian's own life is suddenly put in danger when he is forced to embark on a terrifying boat journey to protect an innocent witness, Sheila Blayne, who possesses evidence crucial to the case. Adrift at sea and unable to make radio contact, they realise that someone is tracking them, someone who will not allow them to reach the mainland alive . . .

In Camera

Gerald Hammond

M
MACMILLAN
LONDON

Copyright © Gerald Hammond 1991

First published 1991 by
MACMILLAN LONDON LIMITED
Cavaye Place London SW10 9PG
and Basingstoke

Associated companies in Auckland, Delhi, Dublin, Gaborone,
Hamburg, Harare, Hong Kong, Johannesburg, Kuala Lumpur, Lagos,
Manzini, Melbourne, Mexico City, Nairobi, New York, Singapore
and Tokyo

ISBN 0-333-55705-0

A CIP catalogue record for this book is available from the British
Library

Typeset by Macmillan Production Limited

Printed and bound in Great Britain by Billing and Sons Limited,
Worcester

One

If Keith Calder had not had such a low threshold of boredom, or even if he had been quite sober that fine Saturday afternoon, this story might have taken a different course.

But his partner, Wallace James, had been removed, protesting, for a tour of visits to his wife's relatives. Molly, Keith's own wife, had been called to the sick-bed of an aged aunt. Deborah, his daughter, was away, competing in the British Ladies' Skeet Championship, while Keith, who would dearly have loved to go with her as coach and camp follower, was left to mind the shop.

In the Square at Newton Lauder, the gunshop and fishing tackle emporium had provided Keith with a good living for more than twenty years, but he detested being stuck behind the counter. Usually, the shop took almost the place of a club where those devoted to the pursuit of bird, beast or fish could meet up and exchange lies about their exploits. But this was the dead season. Summer visitors up for the fishing were more inclined to go and fish than to linger and talk about it, while those locals who should have been bringing in their guns for between-season servicing were, as usual, waiting until the last minute before demanding instant attention and priority, each over the other. To add insult to injury, the weather was fine and the pigeon were dropping in to laid barley. Even from the Square, occasional shots could be heard as the local pigeon-shooters came to terms with the elusive birds. In short, as Keith told his brother-in-law when they met over a bar lunch in the hotel, if God was going to give the year an enema, this was when he would insert the tube. They exchanged large, malt whiskies and toasted the coming season.

Keith crossed the Square and re-opened the shop, feeling slightly less put-upon.

Almost on his heels, a visitor arrived. Keith looked up with relief from some invoices. The arrival was a thin man with a drooping moustache, dressed, despite the weather, in heavy tweeds and a fore-and-aft hat. He might have been a fisherman in search of tackle or a deerstalker stocking up with cartridges for the hill, but Keith recognised the stooped posture, worn hands and narrowed eyes of one who had spent much of his life at the workbench. This would be the visitor whom he had been expecting at some unspecified time in the afternoon.

'Mr Hall?' he said.

'Robert Hall. You'd be Keith Calder?' The accent was unmistakably Midlands, probably Birmimgham.

'I would.' They shook hands. 'I'm on my own this afternoon,' Keith said, 'so we'll have to talk here. I hope we'll be interrupted by a rush of customers but I'm not counting on it.'

Hall smiled nervously, showing uneven teeth. 'I understand.'

'Let's sit down.' There were two bentwood chairs for customers. 'We're quiet just now,' Keith said, 'but I'll be rushed off my feet soon. The managing director of Gunsport thought that he'd pulled off a coup with a bulk purchase of twelve-bore semi-autos, but when they arrived they all had five-shot magazines.'

Hall nodded. Under changed legislation, five-shot semi-automatic shotguns would be virtually unsellable.

'Meantime,' Keith said, 'the importer went bust and decamped – which, of course, is how he'd managed to

8

give Gunsport a thief's bargain in the first place. The manufacturer doesn't want to know, and quoted a crazy price for modification and re-proof. I've got the contract for blocking the magazines down to two-shot, starting in about three weeks at the latest. I couldn't handle the whole of it, even if I had nothing else to do.'

A few minutes spent in discussing the technicalities of carrying out the modification to the satisfaction of the Proof House were enough to convince Keith that Hall could do the job.

'Where would I be working?' Hall asked. He glanced towards the back shop.

Keith smiled. 'I used to work there,' he said, 'but we need it all for storage. I do my gunsmithing at home. I've a workbench upstairs, but there's quite a good little machine-shop set up in a former coach-house. It's about two miles north of the town. You have a car?'

Hall shook his head. 'I don't drive. I came through by train and bus. But it sounds like a pleasant walk, morning and evening. I was put in touch with a Mrs Scott in the town. She told me on the phone that there was a room for me if I wanted it.'

'You're available soon?'

'Right away, if you want me.'

'Would you have any objection to serving in the shop occasionally?'

Hall glanced round the racked guns, fishing rods, waders, decoys and shelf after shelf of cartridges and small gear. He smiled again, more confidently. 'Lord, no! I did a lot of that while I was with Alderkin's. I shoot a little and fish a lot and I get on with people.'

Keith felt a pleasurable glow as he pictured himself freed to get back to his workbench among the antique guns, making a foray with Deborah to decoy pigeons whenever the mood took him. He had already taken up Hall's earlier references and received glowing reports of him. There was no reason not to strike an immediate deal

9

– except that Keith was in no hurry to be left idle in the shop, kicking his heels in the faint hope that some small boy would come in for a penn'orth of maggots.

Keith glanced down at the *curriculum vitae* that Hall had sent him. 'Bruce Ailmer was your most recent employer but I notice that you didn't give his name as a reference. Why did you leave?'

Hall looked uncomfortable. 'Personal reasons,' he said.

Keith felt a stirring of sympathy. Bruce Ailmer of Dundee was a gunsmith in a fair way of business, pulling in more than his fair share of high-quality work, but he was not an easy man to get along with.

'He was your last employer,' Keith said. 'Is there any reason why I shouldn't consult him?'

'I'd very much rather that you didn't.'

Again, Keith nearly left it there. Only his reluctance to break off human contact spurred him on. 'Then I think you'd better tell me about your "personal reasons",' he said.

Hall put up a hand to his moustache and then touched an eyebrow. 'Mr Ailmer can be difficult. He has a temper. We just didn't get along. Can't we leave it at that?' He looked down at his hands.

Keith felt the faint prickling up his spine that always warned him of something untoward lurking in the background. Hall was uneasy, evasive, possibly lying. Keith felt curiosity stir in him – much, he thought, as a mother would feel a baby stir. 'You must see that we can't,' he said. 'The job's yours if you want it, but first you'll have to convince me that you left Ailmer for a good reason. For all I know . . . ' He left the implication hanging in the air.

'But I've explained— '

'You're hiding something,' Keith said.

A woman's heels clicked by outside and a car started up in the Square, but it was very quiet in the shop.

Hall looked up suddenly and met Keith's eye. 'All right,' he said. 'I'll tell you. In confidence?'

10

'That would have to depend. I can't give a blanket promise. But I can hold my tongue when there's no reason to let go of it.'

Hall's drooping frame sagged further. 'I suppose so. What I told you was true enough. Bruce Ailmer's a scratchy sod. He'll find fault with perfectly good work, just to give himself the pleasure of chewing off an employee. I think he enjoys the feeling of superiority. But it was a good enough job, as jobs go.'

'So what went wrong?' Keith asked.

'Nothing went wrong as such.'

'But?'

'Yes, there was a but. Late last week, a woman went in to see the boss – a hag of around fifty, stout but hatchet-faced, with bleached hair and a voice that could have reamed the pitting out of a gun-barrel. He took her into his own room, which is partitioned off from the other three or four workplaces.

'I'd been restoring a pair of barrels. The blueing tank's in a small cellar beneath Ailmer's room and there's not much more than floorboards in between. But there's no window to his room, so he usually has a ventilation fan switched on. He doesn't realise it, but the fan running nearby masks the sound of anybody working in the cellar below, while somebody in the cellar can hear voices above.

'I wasn't listening particularly. In fact, I don't remember hearing a single word Mr Ailmer said. But the woman's voice was penetrating. I only made out a word or two until I heard her say " . . . converted to fully automatic . . . " and something about a "banana clip". That caught my attention all right.'

'It would,' Keith said with feeling. 'Did you hear anything else?'

'Not a lot, but what I did hear scared me shitless. Something about " . . . into the case all right if you shorten the barrel." And " . . . trigger on the outside."

Then, just as she was leaving, I heard her quite clearly. She said, "Payment in American dollars." '

An elderly man chose that moment to come into the shop in search of braided fishing-line. Keith dealt with him expeditiously and sat down again. 'You realise what you were listening to?' he asked.

'I tried not to believe it,' Hall said.

Keith shook his head. 'They had to be talking about an assassination weapon. Turning a rifle into a submachine-gun and fitting it into some sort of case with a trigger accessible from outside.'

'That's what I was afraid of. I tried to think of other explanations to fit the facts. Meanwhile, the boss began staying late and working in his own room. Nothing unusual about that, except that he gave me no idea what he was working on, and it didn't seem to be any of the jobs which were on the books.'

'So, the next time he spoke an unkind word to you, you made it your excuse to quit?' Keith guessed.

'Not immediately,' Hall said. 'Two days later, a turn-screw rolled off the edge and down the back of the cupboard beside my bench. I fished for it with a piece of wire . . . and brought out a section of rifle-barrel complete with foresight. And it didn't come off a model that had been worked on during my time there. From the taper and the gold bead foresight it reminded me of the Ruger ten-twenty-two Sporter.'

Keith shook his head. 'Not the Sporter. It'd be the carbine. No point chopping up the more expensive model when the cheaper one would do the same job. American again, you'll note.'

'Again?'

'She mentioned dollars. Have you been to the police?'

It was Hall's turn for a headshake. 'At first, I was hesitating. If the job turned out to be legitimate – for export with proper paperwork, or for the Government – I could have done myself a whole lot of no good, running

12

to the police to tell tales about my employer. But after I found that piece of rifle-barrel I got really worried. At the time, there was only one other gunsmith working for Ailmer; and he was off work with a hernia. At best, it looked as though Ailmer was preparing to shift the blame onto me if the job was ever traced back to his workshop. At worst, I was going to be set up. God alone knows what other evidence might be hidden about the place.'

'What did you do with the piece of barrel?' Keith asked.

'Hid it under the blueing tank. Then I let one of the usual squabbles blow up into a real row, chucked in my resignation and got the hell out of there. That was the day your advertisement appeared. I phoned straight away. I . . . I'd just as soon that Bruce Ailmer didn't know where I'd gone. If he finds that I've moved the evidence and starts putting two and two together . . . '

'If he does that,' Keith said, frowning, 'the first thing he'll do is to look through the papers to see who was advertising for a gunsmith around that time. The job's yours if you still want it. But I don't like the idea of you walking along the main road twice a day. There are some cottages at the market garden behind my house and I'll ask about a room there. Come to the shop here on Monday morning. Is that soon enough?'

The prospect of a secure future seemed to put new strength into Robert Hall's backbone. He sat up straighter. 'No problem. I left my luggage in Edinburgh. I can spend tomorrow with a friend there and come out on the first bus on Monday.'

'But,' Keith said firmly, 'you can't just put it all out of your mind and forget it. You'll have to go to the police. There's an assassination being planned. We don't know who the target is. It may only be a politician but it could be somebody important.' Keith paused. Something about his last sentence had seemed out of key; but no, it made sense. 'You'll be in a much stronger position, if you really are being earmarked to carry the can, if you get to the

cops first. Conversely, imagine the murder taking place
and it emerges that you and I knew about the weapon.
Both our heads would be on the block. Leave it with
me for the moment, but be prepared to tell it all on
Monday.'

'I suppose you're right,' Hall said sadly. 'In principle,
I know you are. But the thought of telling it all to the
police and then appearing in court and having to stand
up to cross-examination makes my guts feel loose.'

'If it goes that length, tell the absolute truth and
stick to it and you'll be all right. They aren't monsters.
Some of the police and even one or two lawyers really
do have only one head each – my daughter's boyfriend
for one. He's the local Firearms Officer, so he makes a
good starting-point. I'll give him a ring.'

Hall got out of his chair and shook hands firmly. 'I
feel better now,' he said. 'You were right and you've
shown me what to do.'

He left to catch the bus back to Edinburgh and Keith
went to the phone.

Sergeant Ian Fellowes was another who suffered from
Saturday blues. Neither in his function as a detective
sergeant, responsible to Edinburgh for the investigation
of minor crime in Newton Lauder, nor as the local
Firearms Officer was there anything more than the most
mundane of routine duties to occupy his attention; but
the roster insisted that he should be on duty, so on duty
he was.

Keith's phone-call put an end to boredom for good
and all. He quitted his small office with relief, took a
short cut through the Town Hall, crossed the Square to
the old-fashioned frontage of the gunshop and entered,
smiling. He liked Keith. He would have liked the older
man even if Keith had not managed to father the most
companionable, argumentative and generally desirable
girl in the western hemisphere.

14

A brief spurt of business – a small boy wanting cata-
pult rubber and a local keeper in search of decoy sticks –
had died down. The shop was empty of customers again.
Keith's news soon wiped away the smile.

'Where's this man Hall?' Ian asked. 'I'd better see him.'

'Gone back to Edinburgh to collect his luggage,' Keith
said. 'You'll get him on Monday morning.'

Ian Fellowes looked at the man who might some day
be his father-in-law with less than his usual affection.
'For God's sake!' he said. 'Couldn't you have kept him
here?'

'There's no tearing hurry. One man, working on his
own and running a business at the same time, won't turn
a rather mundane rifle into a sophisticated assassination
weapon overnight.'

'That could depend how polished a job he was making
of it,' Ian pointed out.

'If you're in any doubt, you could have Bob Hall
lifted off the bus. Or you could phone Dundee. Tell
them that you've had a tip-off. They could raid Ailmer's
workshop,' Keith suggested hopefully. He had never liked
Bruce Ailmer and the removal of a serious element of
competition was an attractive prospect.

The Sergeant looked doubtful. 'On the basis of a scrap
of rifle-barrel and what you tell me you've deduced from
a few words overheard by some Nervous Nelly who I've
been denied the chance of questioning? No. This goes
through channels,' he said. 'The one advantage of being
a junior officer is that you can pass the buck upstairs
and let your superiors lay themselves open to ridicule
and mirth.'

'Or grab the credit, if it averts an attempted coup.'

'They'd grab it anyway.'

'That's true,' Keith said.

The telephone made bird-like noises. Keith answered
it. Deborah was calling. She had finished as runner-up
after a shoot-off and was on the way home.

15

'Tell her, "Well done!" from me,' Ian said.

Keith relayed the message.

'Thanks. I've spoken to Mum,' Deborah said. 'She was trying to reach you but you must have gone to lunch. Somebody with an American accent wanted to know when you'd be home.'

'I've had a bellyful of our transatlantic cousins for the moment,' Keith said.

They disconnected.

'What went wrong in the shoot-off?' Ian asked.

'A sudden gust of wind, she said. Never mind. There's always next year.'

The danger of a coup d'état suddenly seemed less important. They discussed the prospects for next year for a few minutes.

'I'd better get back and put a report on the wire,' Ian said at last. 'I'll have to put the blame on you for letting the witness buzz off. You don't mind?'

'Not in the least,' Keith said. 'Be my guest. They'll believe anything of me. That bugger McHarg thinks that I invented original sin.'

Ian Fellowes said nothing. Keith's iniquity was the one subject on which he sometimes found himself in agreement with his seniors.

Ian Fellowes spent most of the Sunday with his Deborah. Thoughts of assassinations seldom crossed his mind and Deborah was at first only interested in bemoaning the gust of wind which had set her goal beyond her reach for another year; but he did manage to ask a few supplementary questions of her. Deborah was almost as knowledgeable about firearms as her father and was better able to make allowance for the ignorance of the listener while expounding. Thus before the day was over Ian at least knew what a banana clip might be.

It was on the Monday morning that, as he later expressed it, the Flymo passed over the dog-turd. The

16

first sniff to waft his way came in the form of a phone-call from Keith. Robert Hall had failed to show up to start his new job.

The Sergeant's report had been faxed to Edinburgh but, as a matter of routine, a copy had circulated locally and Chief Superintendent Munro had read it. Although Mr Munro's authority over him was primarily administrative, Ian would not have been surprised if he had been summoned to the presence. Instead, however, there was a token tap on the door and the Chief Superintendent's scrawny figure entered and folded itself into a visitor's chair.

'Sit you down, Sergeant,' Munro said amicably. 'I just wanted a word. That report you put in about the Dundee gunsmith. Have you seen the witness Hall yet?'

The Sergeant tried to hide his anxiety. 'Not yet, sir. Mr Calder's going to phone me whenever he arrives. No doubt he's missed the first bus.'

'No doubt,' Munro said. 'Tell me what you make of the evidence so far. The matter, after all, is still one of crime prevention – and crime prevention is my responsibility, locally.'

'Locally,' the Sergeant said musingly, as though merely repeating the Chief Superintendent's last word.

'That is what I said.' Munro's voice had all the pedantic lilt of the West Highlander plus a sharpness which was forgivable in a Chief Superintendent who had just been reminded of his limitations by an underling. 'We do not know that the planned assassination – if that is what it is – would not be local. The Moderator of the Church of Scotland is to visit here in two weeks' time. So tell me what you think of the evidence.'

The Sergeant had his own opinion as to whether the Moderator would be a worthy target for a professional assassin, but he kept it to himself. 'Mr Hall may have been romancing,' he said, 'but if he told Mr Calder the truth it adds up convincingly. A small rifle, cut down and

17

converted to automatic fire – I'm told that that's a much easier conversion than the other way around – installed in some sort of case, with a trigger worked, probably, from inside the handle and with a "banana clip" – that's a magazine – taking anything up to thirty rounds at a time. Discounting remote possibilities such as that it's intended for use in a James Bond film, it can only add up to a murder weapon, intended to be brought close to somebody who would otherwise be difficult to approach.'

'That is much what I thought myself,' Munro said comfortably and lapsed into silence .

When a minute had passed without another word spoken, the Sergeant said, 'Was there anything else, sir?'

'No, nothing. Carry on with your work. I am waiting for Mr McHarg to phone you, as he surely will.' Mr Munro glanced disapprovingly at his plain, silver wrist-watch. 'Mr McHarg does not keep early hours. When he phones, switch on that little gadget.'

All was now clear. Chief Superintendent Munro and Detective Superintendent McHarg were old acquaintances, rivals and enemies. Each had an unerring instinct for those moments when the other was exposing, or could be induced to expose, his jugular vein. Such moments were not good times for subordinate staff to be around. The Sergeant tried and failed to think of a good excuse to get out of the room, out of the building and preferably out of the country.

But he was still doodling Deborah's lips on the back of a blank firearms certificate when the telephone rang. He snatched it up, hoping against hope that Keith's voice would announce the safe arrival of Robert Hall.

'Sergeant Fellowes?' barked Mr McHarg's voice.

The Sergeant switched on his telephone amplifier. 'Speaking, sir. I have Mr Munro with me.'

'What does the Chief Superintendent want?'

Munro leaned forward towards the amplifier. 'I was

discussing the Sergeant's report about the weapon being built in Dundee.'

'Do you mind if I ask, Hamish, just what the hell it has to do with you?'

'Not at all, Gordon,' Munro said affably. Only two discs of colour, high on his cheeks, betrayed his anger. 'It is a matter of crime prevention.'

'I suppose it would be, at that. All right, sit in if you want. Sergeant, have you seen this man Hall yet?'

'Not yet, sir. He's due in Newton Lauder this morning.'

'According to your report, he was due to start a new job in Newton Lauder this morning. If he existed at all. We have only Calder's word to go on.'

Munro leaned forward again. There was a hint of mischief on his dour countenance. 'Mr Calder has always proved a reliable witness in the past.' He sat back, satisfied that he had planted the needle where it would do most good.

He was not disappointed. 'Reliable! If by that you mean that the courts have sometimes been persuaded to agree with his warped viewpoint, than maybe. The Sergeant may be sweet on Calder's daughter, but you know and I know, Hamish, that the man's sailed so close to the wind, and so often, that he lives in a state of imminent capsize. Tayside police don't have a whore's prayer of a chance of getting a warrant to search the premises of a reputable firm on the basis of hearsay evidence transmitted through that source. Sergeant!'

'Sir?'

'You are not, repeat not, to make any moves in this matter until the man Hall has turned up, if then. In fact, if he exists and shows his face, I'm to be told. I'll see him myself.'

'I gather then,' said Munro, 'that you have no particular need for the Sergeant's services in the immediate future? I was considering sending him on a course on the Firearms (Amendment) Act.'

19

'Good idea,' said McHarg. 'Keep him out of harm's way for a bit. You'll let me know if Hall turns up?'

'I certainly will,' said Munro.

The connection was broken. The Sergeant put down his telephone and switched off the amplifier. He met Munro's eyes and braced himself. Something was coming and he thought that he might not like it.

'You really believe,' said Munro, 'that a serious crime is in train?'

For a moment Ian Fellowes wondered where his best interests lay, but he decided to be forthright. 'I do. And if I may say so, I think you were playing with fire to provoke Mr McHarg into taking the opposite view.'

'Perhaps.' The Chief Superintendent smiled thinly. 'And perhaps I know exactly where I am hoping to put the fire. Mr McHarg should not let himself be so easily provoked. Tell me, Sergeant, are you so sure that a crime is imminent that you'd be prepared to gamble on it?'

Ian thought for a moment and then said, 'Yes. I am.'

'Then so you shall. We both will. You already know more than enough about the Firearms (Amendment) Act. Instead, I am going to give you a week's leave – and more if necessary. If you can come up with some real evidence, it won't count against your annual leave. That is what you gamble. You follow me?'

Sergeant Fellowes nodded without speaking.

'I will put our discussion with Mr McHarg on record. And I'll give you your instructions in writing, to protect you. But if you come up with positive evidence, Mr McHarg will be in no position to make trouble; while, if you do not, he need never know of it. Are you agreeable?'

The proposition was, to say the least, unusual. Sergeant Fellowes frowned. 'May I think about it?' he asked.

'Of course. After all, Mr Hall may still arrive and the matter settle itself one way or the other. Let me know this afternoon and, if you agree, you can make a start in the morning.' Munro paused and dispensed a look which reminded the Sergeant of a mother wondering whether the baby's spots were really only nappy-rash. 'You do understand that this would be unofficial and, being unofficial, there would be little or no back-up? No search-warrant, no phone tapping. I'll make a telephone-call to an old friend in Tayside, off the record, and he'll help if he can. If there's an arrest to be made, call on him. No rough stuff, and for the love of the Almighty no publicity – not, at least, until the case is rock-solid. You understand me?'

'Oh, yes,' said the Sergeant. 'I understand you all right.'

As soon as he was alone, he left his office and went in search of Keith Calder. He urgently needed the advice of one whose experience of bending the rules far exceeded his own.

Two

Ian Fellowes sat in the back of the borrowed van. Thanks to the benevolent interference of the Calder family, he was not uncomfortable. He was seated in an old armchair which had once graced Keith's study. A pair of binoculars was held ready at eye-level by a clamp of the type usually associated with laboratory apparatus but which found an occasional use in Keith's workshop. And at his elbow were a bottled-gas stove and all the necessities for the making of simple snacks. It was the second fruitless morning of his vigil, but a radio, playing softly, helped to relieve the monotony of looking along a street, empty but for parked cars and a few children playing some incomprehensible game, to where the doorway to Bruce Ailmer's workshop faced him from the cross-street beyond a changing screen of vehicles. Between the rooftops, the Tay estuary shone in the bright sunlight.

Behind him, the door of the van slid back softly. Ian jumped and twisted round. His mind had been on weapons and assassination. But the man who climbed in and sat sideways in the driving seat had the calm solidity and the neat haircut that enables one policeman to recognise another.

'Detective Sergeant Fellowes?' said the newcomer. 'DS Bert Angus.' He wrinkled his nose at the atmosphere in the van.

Ian flushed. Twenty-four hours of almost constant vigilance had allowed little time for sleep and none for bathing. 'I was expecting DC Fettes,' he said.

22

'He's helping at a warehouse break-in. You'll have to make do with me.'

'Did Fettes manage to get me a radio?'

'He tried, but there was no way. Officially you're not here at all and the chief doesn't want a lot of messages passed through the Control Room. If anybody collects what you're looking for, follow until you can get to a phone. You need spelled for a while?'

'I've just been for a pee in the pub,' Ian said. 'Hope I didn't miss anything. That Jag wasn't there when I left.'

DC Angus twisted further round and tried to look through the back window of the van which, except for a small strip at eye-level, was coated with a carefully preserved layer of traffic grime. 'Shouldn't think so, if it's still there,' he said. 'All the same, you should have stuck it out – tied a knot in it or something. You knew somebody'd be along. No sign of your girlfriend?'

'Two women have called and come away with gun-cases, but neither answered the description. I put them down as wives collecting their husbands' guns after over-haul.'

Bert Angus nodded. He had an unsmiling face and cold eyes. 'Seems reasonable,' he said. 'My chief told us the background. He said he'd buy Champagne for the whole department if you can get him a good reason to give the place a thorough searching. In our book, Ailmer's been getting away with it for too damn long.'

'Trading in illegal, off-register weapons?'

'You can set that to music. The law gives us a certain right of access, but there's a limit. I told the chief that his chances of one man riding in from out of town and doing a Lone Ranger were less than his chance of winning the pools two weeks running.'

Ian smiled wryly. 'I told Chief Superintendent Munro much the same when I phoned him last night. He said to stick at it.'

'The missing witness hasn't turned up yet?'

'Not as of last night. Probably lost his nerve and done a bunk.'

Angus lit a cigarette, dropped the match on the floor and made a sound intended to convey contempt and disbelief. 'Probably made the whole thing up, to explain why he left his last job in a hurry. Ailmer probably caught him with his hand in the till or trying to muscle in on the illegal arms dealing. Not that that would bother the man Calder. He's tarred with the same brush.'

'That isn't the impression I have of him,' Ian said carefully.

'Around here, his reputation stinks.'

Ian's first instinct was to rush to the defence of the friend who might well become his father-in-law. He bit back some hot words. 'When Mr Calder's consulted by the defence in a firearms prosecution, he can drive a coach and horses through a sloppily prepared case. That doesn't endear him to senior officers.'

'I'm told that his daughter's a looker. You sound as if you've been getting your share.'

For a moment, Ian was lost for a suitably devastating retort. The moment passed for ever when the door of Bruce Ailmer's workshop opened and a stout woman came out.

'There she is,' he said. 'Hatchet face, bleached hair and all. And, by God, I've seen her before! She's carrying a case but the Jag's hiding it.' He grabbed Keith's binoculars but left the rest of his gear to look after itself. The woman entered the front of the Jaguar. 'Get the hell out of the driving seat. No, wait! She's turning this way.'

'Hellfire!' DS Angus said. 'My car's round the corner.'

'Try to catch up. If you lose us, I'll phone your HQ.'

The Jaguar swept past, climbing the steep street. DS Angus got out of the van. 'Right. Or would you prefer I came with you?'

Ian settled into the driving seat and started the van's

engine. 'Two vehicles would be better, in case she has a meet.'

'It's your case. Good luck!' Angus slammed the door and patted the roof.

Ian fed some revs to the engine and let the clutch out. The van fluffed twice and then pulled away with a whine of gears.

The Jaguar was already far up the hill and climbing easily. Ian Fellowes cursed the sluggish van, fought with the gearbox and looked in his mirror. Where the hell was Bert Angus?

A flow of traffic at a mini-roundabout halted the Jaguar. Ian arrived and came to a halt, four cars behind. He could see the woman's head with its tight bright hair-do, nodding impatiently. The column moved out, too soon for DS Angus to come in sight. The Jaguar shot away and Ian clung on, ignoring the Highway Code, the statutory speed limit and the protests from the van's engine just to keep the hurrying vehicle in his sights. He knew Dundee fairly well and thought that she was making for the Kingsway.

Another traffic check enabled him almost to overtake the Jaguar before it crossed above the Kingsway and took a slip road down onto it, heading east. There was a forty limit but the Jaguar ignored it and shot ahead again.

It passed out of sight. But the Kingsway ends in a monster roundabout where seven roads converge and there he saw it waiting while a column of traffic followed a juggernaut up from the city centre and onto the Arbroath road. The Jaguar moved out but Ian was cut off again by renewed traffic. The Jaguar circled past the Arbroath road. City centre? he wondered. Or the Tay Road Bridge? But the Jag turned off between the two main roads, descending at right angles towards the river.

There came another gap in the traffic – less than enough, but Ian forced his way through in a blaring of horns and set off in pursuit. The street had a long name but he went by too fast to read it.

He came down to the small roundabout on the road between Dundee and Broughty Ferry. There was no sign of the Jaguar. He conjured up a faint recollection of the map. The Jag would not have come by this road only to turn right towards the city centre. The minor road ahead led nowhere. He turned left and put his foot hard down, uttering aloud an ill-assorted mixture of prayers and curses which, he thought later, must seriously have damaged his chances of getting into Heaven.

Either the prayers or the curses bore fruit. Just before reaching Broughty Ferry he came over a crest to see the Jaguar, some way ahead, make a slow turn into the driveway of a substantial house. To have braked from that speed might have drawn the woman's attention. He swept past and came to a set of traffic lights which seemed to have stuck at red. When they changed he turned off, drove round a small block and came back to the lights. Red again. Green came at last.

As he approached the house where the Jaguar had turned in, the woman came out of the driveway on foot and carrying a case which looked very much like the one that she had brought out of Ailmer's workshop. Three or four men appeared out of nowhere and followed her, as if by chance. She crossed the road and entered the grounds of the Royal Tay Yacht Club. Ian cruised slowly past the opening. The woman had not entered the clubhouse but was making her way down through the garden towards the River Tay. Three of the men followed at a distance. They were not dressed for sailing.

Sheila Blayne sat uncomfortably on the caravan's tow-bar. The handbrake lever was digging into her hip and she thought that she was probably getting grease onto her new summer skirt.

The small caravan had appeared overnight, parked

26

and apparently abandoned on the very spot where on the previous day she had started her sketch. On seeing it, she had almost decided to abandon her project. But the sketch had progressed with miraculous fluency, developing towards a finished drawing. For once, the mysteries of perspective had resolved themselves and the whole panorama of the Tay estuary receded faultlessly into the distance. The composition also was doing her work for her. A black-backed gull had perched for a moment in the left foreground, just where a point of punctuation was needed. For the first time since she had given up her work as a secretary in order to be reborn as an art student, she felt a rising sense of expectation. This one was going to be good. Good enough to work up into a painting which would certainly impress her tutor. It might even – the ultimate accolade – sell.

Today was calmer than the day before and the sky was cloudless, but no matter. Yesterday, until the heat brought the mist up from seaward, she had concentrated her enchanted pencil on capturing the highlights from the dancing wavelets, the perfect arrangement of the clouds and their shadows on the hills of Fife. Now she hurried to get the rest of the details firmed in with the minimum of deft pencil strokes. The purposeful rigging of the boats lying off the yacht club. The gaunt lines of the two bridges. The fading recession of the distant hills and the crisp skyline of the city.

It was cool in the shade of the caravan but she was half expecting a change and was alerted as soon as the temperature dropped. Behind her the embankment, where the road climbed to cross the railway line, cut off Broughty Ferry and her view towards the lighthouses of Buddon Ness, but by leaning backwards almost to toppling point she could see diagonally across the river and downstream. That damned midsummer haar was rolling in again from the sea. Already Tentsmuir Point was gone and Tayport was about to vanish. Soon she would be forced to quit, as she had the day before. Tomorrow might be overcast or lost in a downpour. Please, God, let her remember the colours. She had taken transparencies with her old Zenith, but a photograph was never quite the same. Her pencil danced on.

With minutes to spare, she thought that she had it all. Half closing her eyes, she studied the whole. It was far and away the best that she had ever done. She had always had the knack of the small drawing, capturing a likeness or expressing a mood. But now, at last, formal training and natural talent had come together. This . . . this was a picture. And yet . . .

Vacillating between elation and despair, she saw that it was a panorama of scenery, competently executed but nothing more. It was a backcloth, a perfect backcloth for foreground figures. About . . . there! She could add them later, making use of the art school models or her fellow-students. But the lighting and the mood would be different. And just what should the scale be, to fit the perspective that had poured off her pencil? The next few lines would make or mar.

A man was walking towards her at the very edge of the water. If he were quick and reached the chosen place before the mist arrived, she could at least mark his height on the paper. She glanced behind her again. Tayport was hidden and the fog-bank was very near.

With her eraser she took out a small length of the shore-line. When she looked again, another miracle had been granted. The man had been joined by a woman and they were perfectly posed on the perfect spot. But more, much more: there was about them a suppressed furtiveness in total contrast with the cleanliness of the scene beyond. They were almost caricatures and yet they were real, neither young lovers nor a stodgy married couple but something indefinably different. Partners in evil, perhaps. She slashed them onto the paper just as they were, the man paunchy and slightly bow-legged; the woman stout and past middle age, standing carefully in her thick brogues on the uneven shingle. All this went down in a rush lest they move as much as an inch. The woman had a case which she was handing to the man, an unusual case, and of its own accord Sheila's pencil caught the act. She might not yet be an artist, but for once her innate talent had lifted her far above mediocrity. The scenery, which had seemed so perfect in its own right, was now a background to a pair of figures which made her give an involuntary shiver. When she showed this to her tutor, he would flip.

The two figures parted. Sheila kept her head down, putting in the last lines and shadings from memory and touching in the shadows which had lain across the shingle. There! It was finished. Any more would risk ruination.

When she looked up, the man was walking towards her. He did not notice Sheila, sitting motionless in shadow, until he was almost on top of her. Then he checked in his stride, set down the case carefully and clenched a pair of fists which more nearly expressed brute power than any that she had ever seen. She was tempted to turn the page and draw those fists.

'What are you doing there?' he demanded. Seen close to, he was still paunchy but he had the power of self-confidence and she could see that his bulk was more muscle than fat.

'Nothing,' she said dully. 'I'm just going. I haven't touched anything.'

'What *were* you doing, then?' His voice was deep and hoarse and faintly accented. American, she thought. Perhaps Canadian or even Australian.

'Just a sketch. You parked your caravan exactly where I was sitting yesterday when I started it. So I sat on your tow-bar for a minute. Just to finish it off. I haven't done any damage.' She knew that she was babbling but she could not stop herself. Aggressive people always had that effect on her. She stood up and began to collect her odds and ends, hastily, hoping to put an end to the clash.

'Let me see that.' He took two more steps and snatched the block out of her hands before she could drop it into her satchel. One glance was enough. 'Shit!' he said.

He put two fingers into his mouth and produced a piercing whistle. Then, before she could utter more than a startled squeak, he snatched up his case and gripped her wrist with the other hand, swinging her around the corner of the caravan with such energy that her feet almost left the sand. The door was open and he bundled her inside and pushed her down on one of the bunks, laying the case more gently on the other.

If this was to be rape, she thought that she would submit with apparent willingness rather than be forced and then strangled. She tried to speak.

'Shut up.'

Sheila heard footsteps and then the woman's broad figure appeared in the narrow doorway. She had to push to get through; the size of her bust would have made turning sideways a useless gesture. 'What's the noise about?' she asked. Her voice was metallic and piercing. The accent could only have originated in Glasgow.

'She was watching us. Look what she's drawn.'

The woman picked up the sketching block from the worktop where he had dropped it and ripped off the top sheet. After a moment, she lifted her eyes. Sheila realised that the two pairs of eyes studying her might differ in size and shape and colour – the man's were narrow and brown and the woman's were a washed-out blue – but they were identical in expression, dispassionate and pitiless. It was at that moment that she knew how deep was the trouble into which she had fallen.

She opened her mouth to scream. The man had been waiting for that moment. He still held her wrist in one hand, but in the other he had been holding, behind his back, a damp dishcloth. Her attempt at a scream died to a nasal groan as he forced the wadded cloth between her

30

teeth. He gathered both her wrists into one big hand.

The woman put her head out of the door and called loudly but, to Sheila, unintelligibly. She turned back and spoke to the man. 'She'll have to go. A casual passer-by might not have mattered. But this one drew us. Even if we took it away from her, she could draw it again. And that's the kind of evidence which stands up in a court of law.'

The man nodded, carelessly, as though what the woman had said was too obvious to be worth stating. The two were still standing, but neither had to stoop for the caravan's roof. 'How and where?' he said. 'What do you think?'

'Here and now. Keep the body in the van and drop it off after dark.'

'Now, hold your horses, Dora!' the man said. 'You're leaving me stuck all day with a dead body? You're the one with the organisation.'

'You're the one with the caravan. And the package. And you've more to lose. There's no evidence against me except her word.'

The man seemed to find some logic in this argument. 'I won't argue with that. Got something to tie her with?' he asked.

The woman opened a handbag, fat like herself, and produced a short length of cord. 'I was a Girl Guide once,' she said with macabre humour.

'What I had in mind,' he said, 'was an accidental drowning.'

Dora thought it over and then nodded. 'Tie her tight, then,' she said. 'By the time she floats again, a few marks won't show. We'll need salt water. Where's your bucket?'

Terror, more than the cloth, choked Sheila as she realised but refused to accept that to them she was no longer a person. She had lost her identity and become no more than an inconvenient piece of meat awaiting the attention of the butcher. But to herself she was still the hub of the universe. It could not, must not, end like this, just when she had begun to find her talents.

Struggling only made the man tighten his grip until she thought that the bones in her wrists would break. She could not even get her weight forward and try to stand. There were curtains over the caravan's windows so that nobody could see her plight. She wanted to plead, to promise a silence as total as they would achieve by killing her, but she could not get her tongue behind the sour-tasting cloth to push it forward and out. Her brain raced but, finding no answers, raced on until, like an engine running wild, she thought that it would burst. One part of her mind realised, with surprise, that another part was praying. She had not taken refuge in prayer since the day, soon after her twelfth birthday, when she had decided that the concepts of religion were an insult to her budding intelligence.

When Dora's squat figure vanished suddenly from the doorway, Sheila thought that the woman had gone for water and wondered desperately whether she could kick over the bucket or cause some other delay during which her prayers might be answered. Even to be raped would be to live a little longer before being drowned in a bucket like a surplus kitten.

A new figure took the woman's place, a man's figure. Sheila took him for another of the enemy and only realised that an answer to her prayers might already have arrived when she was jerked to her feet as her captor swung round.

There was no time for more than an instant of violence, but an instant which lasted for ever in her mind. One blow was struck. Sheila, being of a different build, could only vaguely comprehend how vicious was that blow, but her captor was down on the caravan's floor and making the sound of a whistling kettle approaching the boil.

The newcomer pulled at her elbow. 'Out and run!'

The blaze of hope through her black despair was so blinding that if he had told her to jump off a cliff Sheila would have saved her questions for later. Happily, he had told her to take the action which she most desperately wanted to take. Unbalanced by the cord at her wrists, she stumbled through the doorway into a wall of mist. During her few minutes inside the caravan the haar had arrived, densest at its front.

Clumsy and disoriented, Sheila stepped down onto the woman Dora, who was lying on her back, purple-faced, kicking her legs in the air and showing directoire underwear. When Sheila landed on her stomach, the breath that the woman was struggling to recover was expelled again with a grunt like an antique bulb motor-horn. The sound was repeated after a few seconds as her rescuer followed Sheila into the fog.

Help had arrived before the first man had time to knot the cord on her wrists. The cord was already unwinding and Sheila was managing to shed the last turn of it when her rescuer overtook her and swung her round by the arm. 'This way,' he said. 'I left a van on the main road.'

They seemed to be heading towards the sound of traffic. But there were footfalls ahead, running. Behind was a confusion of shouts. A voice answered from close on their left. They swung away. More voices and another swerve. She thought that they were heading back past the caravan and towards the yacht club. Her companion stopped dead and Sheila bumped into him, winding herself. A figure ran past their front, pale at the limit of visibility; she thought that it carried a pistol but it might have been no more than a pointing finger. More shouting, four voices at least, seeming to come from all around.

Sheila followed her companion with blind trust. He had taken the place of the God whom she had forsworn nearly twenty years before. If she could have seen his face she might have seen, but never believed, that he

33

was as frightened as herself, as lost and as disoriented. But he was always ahead, always leading, dragging her along with apparent confidence.

Just when she was sure that they were about to reach the hard ground in front of the clubhouse, water lapped at their ankles. They stopped.

Shingle was crunching, not far away.

'Can you swim?' he whispered.

Sheila nodded violently. Swimming and drawing were her only talents.

'Follow me. Quietly.'

He waded into the water and she followed. The slope was gradual and the chill of the water rose with agonising slowness. When it reached her body, the shock quenched her rising hysteria. And she thought that there was taking place another cleansing. She was sure that at some stage she must have been incontinent, but the salt water was removing any traces. The current was trying to push her to her left, towards the sea.

When the water reached her bosom she lifted her feet and struck out, but before she found her rhythm she made one clumsy splash and the voices broke out again on the shore behind them.

Ian Fellowes had led the way into the water unthinkingly, as a blind retreat from the dangers ashore and out of an atavistic instinct to cover his scent. If he had not been subjected to as terrifying an ordeal as had Sheila, he was more aware than she of the nature of the opposition. He was prepared to swim across to Tayport, or at least to try, or to let the tide carry them down to Barry Sands. Almost certainly, he would have drowned them both. But a small yacht appeared out of the mist, one of the many which lie off the yacht club in summer. It was moored, but as the ebb carried them down it seemed to be forging ahead.

He hauled himself over the stern, using the rudder as a step and the small outboard motor which was canted at the transom as a handhold. Sheila was almost swept past, but he grabbed her wrist and hauled her after him. He hoped that any sound they had made had been covered by the noise of the traffic still moving, although gropingly, along the Dundee road.

Sheila collapsed wetly onto one of the cockpit seats, rubbing her arms. Strong men had been dragging her around by the wrists all day, it seemed. She tried to speak but nothing came out and she thought that her vocal cords must be frozen with fear.

Ian had thought that he would never smile again; or not, at least, until he was safely home and in his own bed with the blankets over his head. But he smiled now. He put a finger to his lips and then leaned down and pulled the dishcloth out of her mouth.

She forgot to feel stupid in the relief of getting her voice back. 'Who are you?' she asked. 'Where did you come from?'

'Fellowes. Ian Fellowes. I was under the caravan when you were grabbed. Keep your voice down.'

'Who are those people? They're . . . evil,' she whispered.

'I know it. Talk later. I think we'd better get out of here. I heard somebody say "boat". If they've gone to steal or borrow an inflatable from the Royal Tay, we could find ourselves back in deep trouble. Well, one thing about sail, it's quiet.'

'There's hardly any wind,' she said.

'There'll be more. Trust me.'

She sat and shivered while he went forward. He seemed to blur as he got further away and it was not only the effect of the mist. She put her hand up and realised that, somewhere along the way, she had lost her glasses.

Ian Fellowes stripped the cover off the mainsail. He studied the halliards for a few seconds and then, slowly and as quietly as he could manage, he raised the sail. The blocks were well greased and there was hardly a rattle but

35

the sail slatted gently in the faint breeze. He had expected a gaff rig and the high peak of the gunter mainsail puzzled him for a moment, but he solved the geometric problem and hauled the sail tight and flat. It filled and the boat began to forge slowly ahead. He moved to the bow and took the loop of the mooring off the sampson-post. As he lowered it towards the water the boat's movement brought it taut and he had to let it drop with a small splash.

'Hear that?' snapped a voice from the shore, muffled but discernible.

Ian padded back to the cockpit in his wet socks. He had kicked off his shoes. Sheila looked down and realised that she had done the same, unconsciously. Ian put the helm down and looked at his watch. Sheila felt the promised breeze on her cheek. Ian held the tiller with his knee and sheeted the boom in, inch by inch. Water began to chuckle softly under the bow. To Sheila, the few degrees of heel felt precarious yet vaguely exciting.

'Where are we going?' she asked. 'Tayport?'

He hesitated and used the moment to trim the sail again. 'We're going as far away as I can manage and as quickly as we can. I've only seen pistols so far, but I've reason to believe that they have some heavier armament. Do you happen to know when high tide is? Or was?'

Sheila was pleased to be helpful for once. 'About an hour ago.' She noticed for the first time that her watch had stopped.

'You're sure?'

'I noticed, because I drew the boats the way they were lying and then the things went and turned round. It was nearly an hour later than yesterday.'

'That sounds about right,' Ian said, reassured. He looked at his watch again. 'In which case, we couldn't make Tayport even if we could find it. I used to sail this coast, years ago, in my uncle's yacht. The whole of the Tay basin has to empty through the bottleneck between Tayport and Broughty Ferry.'

Such considerations were beyond Sheila's experience, but it seemed to be a good time for rational discussion. 'The wind seems to be the other way. Wouldn't it push us against the tide? Or have I lost my sense of direction?'

He looked up at the swell of the mainsail. 'Half this breeze only exists because the tide's carrying us down through the air. If we turned, it would drop. We could anchor, but I don't much fancy having the fog blow away suddenly and expose us. They'll have laid hands on a boat by now. And the public can be amazingly blind to what's happening out on the water.'

He fell silent. Sheila could see that he was thinking hard, so she waited. 'We could try to slip ashore further down,' he said at last. 'But that's what they'd expect us to do. And from what I remember, it's mud-banks all the way. For the moment, we'll go all the way down with the tide.' He looked at his watch again. 'Time to go about now, or we'll run aground where the Pile Light used to be.'

Sheila had been riding along on the crest of her relief after her ordeal. But now that she could see again the prospect of a future she also felt the need to know what it might hold. 'Who and what are you, Ian Fellowes?' she asked. 'I know your name, but where do you come from? And what's going on?'

Ian put the boat about and steadied her on a new course. 'Have patience a little longer,' he said. 'I know that it must be driving you up the wall not to know what's happening and why, but could you hold her steady for a few minutes? Keep the breeze where it is. If the sail starts to flap, pull the stick towards you. I'll see if this old tub boasts a compass and a decent foresail. We could use some more speed. He's locked his cabin doors but the forehatch is loose.'

'We seem to be getting along all right,' Sheila said doubtfully. The idea of speeding through the milky vapour was nightmarish.

'We need enough way to get out of the channel in a hurry if a ship comes groping along by radar and echo-sounder. Or to take evasive action if your friends come close.'

'What about the motor?'

He glanced at the rusty outboard and curled his lip. 'Just for the moment, I'd rather hear than be heard.'

Three

Sheila found herself alone and in control of a boat under sail. At first, she expected her least mistake to cause capsize or worse. They were sailing towards a wall of impenetrable fog in which all sorts of unimaginable dangers might lurk. But the wall of fog always receded, remaining a constant fifty yards or so ahead of the bow, taking with it whatever obstacles it might be hiding. Suddenly, the boat was friendly and responsive.

What seemed to be an enormous sail ran up the forestay. Ian padded back and sheeted it in. The boat took on a new angle of heel and picked up more speed. To Sheila, they seemed to be churning along, almost flying. She let worry slip away and concentrated on following instructions. Despite fear and discomfort, she was beginning to enjoy herself. Within a single day, a drab and monotonous life had been transformed. Her art had taken a leap forward. She had been rescued from dire peril by a heroic male figure. And now she was being introduced to a unique new sensation, control of a boat under sail. New horizons, she was sure, were opening beyond her restricted vision. She would almost have welcomed another adventure, provided that it was not too dangerous.

Ian Fellowes was looking around, trying to pierce the white vapour.

'Where are we?' Sheila asked.

'If we see a buoy soon, I'll tell you. If not, we're

lost.' At that moment a conical buoy came out of the mist, seeming to slide across their bows. 'This is where we are,' he said. 'We're here.'

It was not much of an answer, but she awarded it a subdued giggle. There were other things on her mind. 'I'm cold,' she said.

'You must be. Come to think of it, so am I. Keep steering for a little longer.'

He looked at his watch again and vanished down the forehatch and she heard him rummaging around in the cramped space below. When he came up again he had shed his jacket and possibly his other wet clothes and had dragged on a set of paint-stained overalls. He used a small wooden box to weigh down a folded chart and beside it he dropped an untidy bundle of clothes and a coil of cord with tags and tassels.

She handed back the helm almost with reluctance. The bundle of clothes comprised a pair of jeans, a thick and oily sweater, socks, a blanket and a suit of oilskins.

'He's a big lad, whoever he is,' Ian said. 'But at least they're dry clothes and something to keep the breeze out. Go below, if you can manage while folded double. Or you can change under the blanket. I won't look.'

'I'm not much of a peep-show anyway,' she said humbly. She tried to run her fingers through her hair. 'Do we have any fresh water? I'd like to wash the salt—'

'Hush a minute!' They both listened. But there was no sound except for the sluice of their progress and the occasional mew of a gull. 'I'm beginning to imagine things,' he said.

He faced forward, steering his course by the wind, while she squeezed herself into the aft corner of the cockpit, jammed between the tiller and the coaming and, half-seated, struggled out of her sodden dress. It felt daring to undress with a man only inches away. She had dropped her wet dress on the cockpit sole when the sound which had alerted him came again. A motorboat engine could be heard, steady on the port bow but growing louder.

Holding the mainsheet blocks to prevent a rattle, Ian put the boat about. It was impossible to keep his back to Sheila and if it had been possible it would have been irrelevant. Sheila's first reaction was chagrin, that he should glimpse her in her sensible underwear. Why was she always doomed to be unglamorous? She could have been wearing something feminine in clinging silk. Even to be nude would have been less of a humiliation. Then, as danger dawned on her, she thought that she would drown herself rather than be delivered again into the hands of that inhuman duo. Hastily, she dragged on the jeans and sweater.

They ghosted back across the channel. The sound of the motorboat crossed their stern. Ian went about again. The sound pottered across their bow and down the other side. Twice, the engine noise stopped and her terror rose again, clamping her jaw and stealing the strength of her limbs. She could imagine men, evil men with weapons, listening for her heartbeat. Ian held the boat steady, the sails neither slatting nor fully filled. The noise of the engine began again. It faded away upstream.

Ian Fellowes let out his breath. 'Much virtue in silent travel,' he said. If her vision had been sharper, she might have seen that his hand was shaking.

'Perhaps it was somebody who could have helped us.'

'Not a chance,' he said. 'They were making a searching pattern. And they stopped their engine to listen.'

'They could have been looking for a stolen boat. This boat.'

'If the mist's still holding, back there, the owner won't know it's missing yet. Unless the wrong people have told him.' He shrugged. 'But that's just my guess. Next time around, do you want to make the decision?'

Sheila opened her mouth to deny any such wish, but

she had lost his attention. A faint shape hardened in the mist. It became another buoy.

'Lady Shoal.' He adjusted the course slightly. 'There's a short cut through Abertay Sands but I wouldn't try it in this mist. Anyway, I think we've already gone past it.' He had taken a grid compass from the wooden box and fitted it to a bracket at the front of the cockpit. He began a series of computations involving his watch, the compass and the chart.

'Are you still busy?' Sheila asked a few minutes later. 'Or is this an okay time to talk?'

Ian looked up from the chart. 'Provided the next two buoys show up where they should, I think the immediate panic's over. Go ahead.'

They stole a moment to glance at each other, awareness becoming observation. She was not the old prune he had thought her at first. He saw a thin woman, although at some time he had noticed that she was far from flat-chested. Even with her hair tangled and plastered to her skull, she was not without a sort of anxious charm, her femininity enhanced by dependence. She had left the fullness of youth behind, but that loss was offset for the moment by the childish effect of the too-large clothes with the turned-back sleeves and legs. She could have been a teenager who had dressed in Daddy's clothes for an impromptu cabaret. His best guess was that she was around thirty.

Sheila, for her part, noticed that her rescuer was not, as she had thought, eight feet tall; nor was he handsome. He was slightly over average height and no more than passable even by Sheila's undemanding standards. But her eye, biased by thankfulness, chose to ignore a small pimple beside his nose, the stubble on his cheeks and that his sandy hair, as it dried, was sticking up in tufts. Instead, she took note of the firm jaw, the kindly smile and the occasional twinkle in the nervous blue eyes.

'What did you do to that woman?' she asked.

42

'Nothing that I'm proud of,' he said. 'It seemed to be an occasion for forgetting that I was brought up to be gentle with ladies.'

'You needn't be ashamed. Nothing would have been too bad for her. She was talking about drowning me in a bucket, as if it was the most natural thing in the world. You saved my life,' she said, 'and I'm grateful. But don't you think I should know why I was in danger, and why I'm being carried out to sea by a man I never met before? I can't believe that you're telling yourself, "Once aboard the lugger".'

He laughed for the first time, a deep chuckle which somehow pleased her. 'This isn't a lugger, it's a sloop,' he said. 'And, believe me, you're only a small corner of a larger and rather nasty picture.' He broke off. The beat of heavy engines sounded from ahead. He put the helm up and eased the sheets to nurse the boat across the wind.

'If it's a ship they could help us,' she said.

'They could run us down. A wooden boat with a wooden mast hardly shows up on radar at all, especially if the radar's still adjusted to avoid wave-clutter.' He listened. The steady pulse was definitely drawing astern. Soon a grey outline loomed through the mist and vanished again. He brought the boat back on course. 'Cargo of timber. He'll be going in to Tayport.' He looked at his watch again. Sheila wondered how sailors had ever managed to travel the seas before watches were invented. 'He'll have to lie off until the tide makes again,' Ian said. 'I'm just as happy not to be aboard. I suspect that we've made the Tay too hot for ourselves . . . Hey, I think we're coming out of it!'

At first, she thought that he was referring to the river. Her unfocused vision could hardly perceive that their horizon was moving outward, from fifty to a hundred and then two hundred yards. Then, it seemed instantaneously, the sun was through and the sea danced and sparkled to the east. Astern, all view up-river was still shut off. The

43

sea-breeze which had shifted the fog also pressed the sails and the boat chortled along with renewed zest.

Ian pointed to a slender pencil which stood up on the port bow. 'The whistle buoy,' he said triumphantly, as if this should have told Sheila all that she needed to know. 'Hold her steady for a minute.'

He vanished again through the forehatch, leaving Sheila to wonder whether he might not be giving himself time to concoct a story. She narrowed her eyes, trying to keep the buoy in focus. Once she lost sight of it and had to search desperately until she discovered that it seemed to have moved round to the side. She brought the boat back on course.

A minute or two later, the main hatch slid back and the low doors between the cabin and the cockpit were pushed open. 'Soup coming up,' Ian said. 'While the kettle boiled, I thought I'd unscrew the lock. There's some fresh water and a towel of sorts, if you want to rinse your hair.'

It seemed to Sheila that, of the three things she wanted most in the world, to wash the salt out of her hair took pride of place, before even soup or answers to her questions. She hung head-first over the cockpit coaming while he poured water through her hair from a plastic carrier. She dried it with a grubby towel and, while the sun and the breeze finished the drying, teased at it with a comb from the cabin between sips of what was surely the finest soup in the world.

They had passed the whistle buoy, which had produced no more than a feeble yip while they were within earshot. Ian set a new course on the grid compass and eased the sheets. The boat's dance changed from a quickstep to a very slow foxtrot.

'You're some sort of policeman, aren't you?' Sheila said.

'Good guess.'

'MI Five? Or Six?'

44

He chuckled again. 'Nothing so romantic. Just a humble detective sergeant from an outpost of Lothian and Borders.'

Sheila looked at him doubtfully. 'That doesn't sound much like what you've been doing today,' she said. 'Does a detective sergeant from around Edinburgh usually get into fights near Dundee? Or are you off duty?'

'It hasn't been as typical a day as I'd have liked it to be,' he admitted. 'I'll try to explain. I'm based in the Borders under a Superintendent in Edinburgh. We had a tip-off that somebody in Dundee was into something that he shouldn't. My chief mistrusted the source and told me to take no action. But the Chief Superintendent of the local division took a different view. He fiddled my absence and told me to go and take an unofficial look.'

'That still doesn't sound like the police at all,' Sheila said. 'I think you're a private eye.'

'I'm a detective sergeant,' he said patiently. 'Try to think of me that way.'

'I'll try,' she said. 'But you're asking me to take your word for an awful lot. How do I know that you're a goody and not a rival baddy?'

The choice of words made him smile. He left her in charge of the helm again and went below to fetch his identification card.

She screwed up her eyes and satisfied herself that the photograph corresponded with his features. 'All right,' she said. 'You're a detective sergeant.' Or else, she thought, his cover had been well prepared. She watched a lot of television in her lonely studio flat. 'Do you know who those people were?'

'Yes, I know who they were. I suppose it's too much to hope that they don't know who you are?'

'Oh, my God!' she said. 'They must do. I left my bag back at the caravan.' She stopped short. 'What happened to my drawing?' Her eyes filled with tears. The idea of

45

losing the evidence of her burgeoning talent was more awful than the threat to her life.

'It's safe,' Ian said quickly. 'No need to turn on the waterworks. I picked it up and it was in my pocket. I've spread it out to dry, below. It's not exactly pristine.'

'Thank heavens, whatever state it's in! If I've got the original, I can always repeat it.' She was suddenly anxious to get back to real life and work. 'Does it really matter if they know who we are? Surely we've only got to get ashore and contact the police. We could turn back—'

'Back I am not turning,' he said. He gripped the tiller as if afraid that she would wrest control from him. 'I will turn coat, turtle or blue in the face, but not back. That's about the only irreversible decision I've taken so far.' He studied her, weighing her up. She touched her drying hair, thinking that she must look like a golliwog. When he sighed, she was sure of it. 'I'd made up my mind not to tell you anything,' he said at last. 'I thought that you might be safer in ignorance. But if it'll convince you that we're in danger . . . let me see if I can get this across to you. Cast your mind back to the caravan.'

'I'd rather not,' Sheila said with a small shiver.

'Hang onto that emotion for a minute. It may help you. This thing is big and, as you said, those folk are evil. You saw and recorded two people meeting who should not have met.'

At first avoiding names or other clues to the identity of the participants, he told her the story which had come from Robert Hall and the reasons for believing that a weapon of assassination had been commissioned. 'I recognised the woman,' he went on. 'She's bad news. The other man was probably the client. He must have approached her as go-between to get him the weapon, and you saw it being delivered.'

'They decided to kill you, but you got away. Our survival may be disastrous for them. And they can call on all the resources of money and men that they need.

In the woman's case, she can whistle up the sort of hard men who would kill either or both of us for a tenth of the price which she's probably put on our heads by now. Am I frightening you?'

'You are, rather.'

'Good. That's what I'm trying to do.'

'But who are these people?' she persisted. 'It makes it worse, not having an identity to put to them.'

'Why?'

'The bogey-man isn't so frightening when you know that he's only a burglar.'

Ian glanced up at the set of the sails. There was some sense in what she said. 'Well,' he said at last, 'you know so much already that I don't think knowing a little more would increase the danger. Her name is Braddle. Dora Braddle. And she's a very tough cookie. I'm inclined to put a lot of distance between her and ourselves. That's why we're heading south. If we go north there are very few harbours, lots of cliffs and an easily watched coast. I think we've more chance of landing unseen in the Forth.'

'Go on about Dora Braddle,' Sheila said. The woman had for her some of the awful fascination of a snake or a hairy spider.

Ian looked around the horizon while he tried to re-collect the details, told to him by an unusually garrulous inspector whom Ian had been assisting on a case in which the remote hand of Dora Braddle was suspected.

'Dora started life in accountancy,' he said. 'She moved to a stockbroker's office. She had one eye for finance and another for a fiddle, and at that time she wasn't as adept at covering her tracks as she became later. So she got the heave. Then she took up with Danny Bruce.'

'I've heard that name,' Sheila said, pleased to be back among names which were not totally alien. 'It was in the papers. Didn't he go to prison?'

'He did. He was a fence in a very big way of business, in Glasgow, and a very careful man. When he slipped at last and went inside, Dora got together with Danny's daughter Mary, who's a real chip off the old block, and they cooked up a new version of an old racket.

'Danny left his daughter in charge of his legitimate businesses, a string of antique and junk shops. The two ladies seem to have rebuilt the illegal side as a new-style operation, a combination of fencing and money laundering.'

'Money what?' Sheila wanted to grope for a non-existent pencil and to draw a cartoon of the fat woman, washing bank notes in a wooden wash-tub and hanging them on a fence to dry. Her mind was sometimes subject to fits of levity, which she was quite unable to control.

'I'm trying to explain,' Ian said patiently. 'The problems of the successful crook are only beginning when he's grabbed the goods. The little crook either gets ripped off by the fence or sells the stuff for peanuts in the pub the same evening. The bigger man, swindling on a large scale or stealing to order, gets a bigger percentage but then he has a problem explaining his affluence. If the police see a sudden improvement in his lifestyle shortly after a robbery bearing his hallmark, they want a damned good explanation of where the money came from; and the courts are becoming less credulous about gambling wins. Yet you can see the problem from the law's viewpoint. Once money's been juggled a few times, is it still the same money? To put it at its simplest, you have a hundred quid, you steal another hundred and you spend a hundred. Which hundred do you still have?

'Multiply that by many thousands and you begin to get some idea of their operations. The two ingenious ladies set up or bought up a whole string of companies, here, abroad or in offshore oil, mostly paper companies but some small ones with real capital and activities. If somebody has something in need of discreet disposal – bullion, art treasures, jewellery or what have you – it goes in at one end and out at the other end pop shares in BP or the deeds to a house.'

Without losing sight of her apprehensions, Sheila was diverted by this glimpse into a new world of affluence and adventure. 'The money still had to have originated from somewhere,' she said.

'True. And that was where Dora's ingenuity came in. As one example among many, but an example which I know about because it impinged on a case where I was used as a dogsbody, it seems to be widely known in certain quarters that if you're old and infirm and short of assets you can go to Dora and pick up a piece of money or a place in a nursing home in exchange for signing a blank will form, before witnesses of her choosing. Then, when you shuffle off this mortal coil – surprise, surprise! – it turns out that you had thousands in an unsuspected safe-deposit or owned a large house in a good neighbourhood, all bequeathed to your unfortunate old friend who, by coincidence, is so unjustly suspected of having opened Cartier's safe.

'So much for Dora,' he added.

'And the man?'

'Him we don't know. I wish to God we did. American from the sound of him. He might be another intermediary, but from his reaction to your sudden appearance I'd put him down as the hit-man. Nor do we have any idea who the target might be.'

Ian broke off. Visibility was patchy as the sun and the wind toyed with patches of mist, but where they were it had extended to about a mile, giving an illusion of a day clear but for a slight haze, so that a yacht on a reciprocal course, instead of lifting over the horizon, appeared to be born, full-rigged and with colourful spinnaker set, less than a mile away. Soon the two boats were abeam. The helmsman waved cheerfully as they passed.

'I hope he's not going into the Tay,' Ian said. 'He's only got to cast up at Broughty or thereabouts and he'll

49

sure as hell be asked whether he crossed with *Lonely Lady*.'

'Is that this boat's name?' Sheila asked quickly. 'How do you know?'

'Read it on the stern as we climbed aboard. He was a bit far out to be heading for the Tay. If he's going on to Arbroath or Montrose they'll still get to him, but it'll take longer.'

'Where are we going?' Sheila asked. 'No, first tell me how you came to be under the caravan.'

'All right. That, after all, is the easier of the two questions.

'I was watching the gunsmith's workshop. It was a thin chance but the best I could do. We had a description of his woman client. It didn't ring any bells at the time, but I recognised Dora as soon as she came out and a whole set of chimes started ringing. One of the Dundee officers was with me but I lost touch with him when I took off after her. And I don't have a radio – I was told not to go through any Control Rooms.

'Dora drove to Broughty Ferry, parked in the grounds of a house and walked over to the yacht club, escorted by several men, and went down towards the shore. The escort, I suppose, was in case her client decided to accept the weapon without parting with the cash. I found another way down and watched from a distance. I didn't dare to go to a phone in case I lost track of her.

'She strolled around, looking at her watch from time to time. I was sure that she was planning to meet somebody. When I saw the haar rolling in, I thought I'd better get closer. Nobody was looking, so I crawled under the caravan. I was right at the back end and I didn't even see you. When the man first spoke to you, I thought he was talking to me. I nearly answered him. The rest you know.'

Sheila might be unversed in the ways of the underworld but she was not without intelligence. 'Let me see if I've

50

got this straight. That man was a professional killer with a – what do they call it? – a contract?'

'Or a courier taking the weapon to the contract killer. Those are the only two explanations I've been satisfied with so far.' He was frowning, but not at Sheila. 'I should have grabbed the weapon while I had the chance.'

'We'd have drowned,' she pointed out. 'I'm sure that the man was the killer and that the killing's to be in Britain,' she said positively.

'How on earth do you figure that?'

'My turning up put the cat among the pigeons.' Sheila spoke slowly, fumbling to turn her intuitive reasoning into logic. 'But it was the man who grabbed me first. If he was only a courier who was going to take the weapon abroad, I don't see him hanging about and taking the risk of disposing of a witness. And why would Dora Whatsit get involved?'

'If the target was a big enough figure – a President, a Prime Minister or the figurehead of some sectarian body – your sketch could be a deadly threat to both of them.'

Sheila thought in silence. The tale hung together well as far as it went, but would a humble detective sergeant from the outer reaches of some other constabulary be pursuing the villains on his own?

'I've got it,' she said. 'You're Interpol, aren't you?'

'No, I am not! That's your least likely guess yet. Interpol's only a centre for the exchange of intelligence.'

'Special Branch, then?'

Ian's denial was as vehement as if she had suggested that he was a talent scout for the white slave trade. 'Believe whatever you want to believe,' he added. 'At least you can't doubt that I'm on the side of the good guys.'

That seemed indisputable. Sheila certainly counted herself as being one of the good guys and he had proved to be on her side. But, from her occasional reading of spy fiction, it seemed to Sheila that even the good guys were prone to sacrificing the occasional pawn. She decided not to put the thought into his mind.

They thought their own thoughts for a minute. The yacht rode easily through a short seaway coming in from the east. They seemed to have the sea to themselves but that was an illusion created by the lingering haze. The beat of large engines reached them from seaward and later a succession of waves marked the wash of some vessel.

'So where do we go now?' Sheila asked suddenly. 'Have you thought about that?'

'I've thought about nothing else, in between answering your questions,' Ian said. 'Would it help if I did my thinking aloud?'

'Yes. Of course it would.'

'You may not like some of it. Dora and her friend may have said "Oh, the hell with it!" and gone home, but I wouldn't want to bet my life on it, would you?'

Sheila shook her head.

Ian pulled a face. 'I wish now that I'd spoken to that yacht that crossed with us. At least we could have asked him not to mention us, and have given him a message to pass along. I must be going gaga in my old age.'

'The best ideas always arrive too late,' Sheila said comfortingly.

'Thank you for that much. Now, every thug in the country had some business with Dora or is likely to need a favour at some time in the future. And she must know more guilty secrets than St Peter. So we must assume that she can call on all the help she needs. And so we can't just wander ashore and drift around looking for a phone or the nearest police station.

'Northward was a bad risk, a rugged coast overlooked from a main road and few harbours. And we don't have enough food and water for a long trip. But south of here we have dozens of bays and anchorages within a day's sail.

God, how I wish we had a phone-book aboard and a copy of the Yellow Pages!'

The change of subject took Sheila aback, just when she thought that she was coming to grips with the problem. 'But we don't have a telephone. Or do we?' she added. Agents, she knew, were equipped with all sorts of devices for communication.

'No, of course we don't,' Ian said, trying vainly to mask his impatience. The damned woman still seemed to think that he was James Bond. 'But the books might help me to choose the right harbour, one with telephones and police but without the sort of harbourmaster who could already have been reached by phone with some message or other. Something like, "I'm trying to reach an old friend to break bad news to him. If you get sight of *Lonely Lady*, say nothing and phone this number and there's a hundred quid in it for you." '

Sheila would never have thought of anything so devious. 'Do you think that's what they're doing?'

'It's what I'd do. We're crossing St Andrews Bay just now. St Andrews would be the first place they'd think of. I could take us into the Eden and up to Guardbridge, but the main road to St Andrews runs beside the Eden estuary.

'Round the corner into the Forth we've got the Neuk of Fife and a whole string of harbours from Crail onward. And every damn town has a harbourmaster who'd be on the phone before we could get inside and bribe him not to. And in most of them, we'd be stuck on the mud at low tide. We might make it to the police station before they caught up with us, but would you feel safe in the local cop shop with one unarmed man on duty and the other out on patrol?'

Sheila shook her head decisively. An unarmed policeman would be little deterrent to the pair who had dragged her off the beach. 'But we've got to get ashore before we starve,' she pointed out.

'That's for sure,' he agreed. 'What's more, the longer we skulk out here the more chance they have of getting word from some passing skipper and organising a reception. I think we've got to get further south. Dora's city-bred. I don't know about the man, but I don't think he'd be boat-oriented. They'll think of the shore and the local phone-book. To them, Dunbar's a hell of a long way from Dundee, which indeed it is by road. But it's only a short sail across the mouth of the Forth estuary.' He broke off, looked at his watch again and listened. From off the starboard bow, out of the haze came a mournful bellow. 'North Carr light vessel,' he said. He set a new course on the compass. 'We'll take a rest in the anchorage at May Island and head into Dunbar in the early morning. Could you steer a compass course while I make a meal? Shout if you get into difficulties or if you see or hear anything. Anything at all.'

Four

Keith Calder filled the tank of his jeep with unleaded at the Newton Lauder Filling and Service Station, looked at his tyres, decided that they would do until next time and went in to present his credit card to the girl at the till. When he came out into the afternoon sunshine, Chief Superintendent Munro's official Ford Granada was parked on the forecourt and his driver was under the bonnet, in discussion with one of the mechanics.

Munro himself emerged from the toilet and caught sight of Keith. He hesitated and then walked to meet Keith at the jeep. 'A word in private,' he said.

'Hop in.'

Keith's daughter was in the passenger seat. At a nod from her father she moved and curled up in the back with the two dogs. The men seated themselves in the jeep and Keith drove off the pump-apron and parked beyond the Granada.

'I don't know what you want with this toy car,' Munro said peevishly.

'It's cheap to run,' Keith said. 'And I'd back it against that thing of yours, across country. What did you want a word about?'

'A man came to see me this morning. An American. He saw the firearms staff first, but with Sergeant Fellowes away they couldn't deal with him, so they sent him to me. He was asking for the Big Cheese. Is that what I am around there? The Big Cheese?'

55

'The very biggest. What did he want?'

'A firearms certificate for a pistol. To carry. For self-defence, of all things.' Munro's voice was shrill with indignation. 'He said that he was a retired policeman and he'd made a lot of enemies.'

Keith was nodding. 'That follows,' he said. 'And you told him that it was the business of the police to protect him but that they couldn't do it and he wasn't allowed to protect himself. So it was up to him to get killed, after which you would become interested and exact revenge on his behalf?'

'Yes,' Munro said. 'I mean, no. It is getting beyond anything, Keith, when you twist a man's words before he has even uttered them. I certainly told him that he would not get a certificate to carry a firearm for reasons of self-defence.'

'Not even a retired American cop?'

'Especially not a retired American cop. He will be accustomed to carrying a gun, using it first and explaining to a Board of Enquiry afterwards. We do not do things that way.'

'I'd noticed,' Keith said.

'I thought I would warn you,' Munro said. 'He may call on you at the shop. His name is Cardinal. And if I discover that he has got his hands on a pistol, I shall be very interested in finding out where he got it from. You understand me?'

'Somebody with an American accent was trying to reach me the other day. But I'll be good,' Keith said lightly.

'Have you heard from Ian Fellowes?' Deborah asked from her nest between the dogs.

Munro looked sideways at Keith. 'I keep forgetting that he is sweet on young Deborah here. He told you of his . . . errand?'

'Who do you think fixed him up with the van?'

'I should have known. Perhaps we should have this conversation in private.'

'I've no secrets from Deborah,' Keith said.

'And I know that we can trust your discretion. To tell the truth,' Munro said, 'I am concerned.'

'You're what?' Deborah said from the back.

'I think that you heard me. Your boyfriend reported last night, after a day spent in unproductive observation. But this afternoon, my contact at Tayside police phoned me. A woman, answering the description given to you by your witness, collected something from Ailmer's workshop. One of my contact's men was with the Sergeant at the time, but lost touch with him. The van has been found near the Royal Tay Yacht Club, causing a dangerous obstruction in the main road where I'm told they have a sea-fog. There seems to have been some sort of a stishie on the foreshore below the yacht club and two boats are missing, a yacht and one of those inflatable dinghies.'

'And no sign of Ian Fellowes?' Keith asked.

'Not for the moment. And I am gravely concerned.'

'So you should be,' Deborah said.

'Yes. If the Sergeant has not obtained any useful evidence, and if it should come out that I sent him there against the orders of his immediate superior, I could be open to criticism.'

'And I would be leading it,' Keith said. 'Can I give you some advice?'

'Why not? I have given you plenty, over the years. Not that you have ever taken any of it.'

'Well, you'd better take this to heart. Your feud with McHarg will damage both your careers, one of these days. That wouldn't bother me a whole lot. But – it's my turn to utter a warning – if you let it get Ian Fellowes into danger or trouble, you'll have me to answer to as well as the Disciplinary Board.'

'And me,' Deborah said hotly. 'Especially me. I think you've got a nerve, Mr Munro, sending Ian alone and unarmed after an American hit-man and then worrying about your own reputation. If anything's happened to Ian, I'll . . . I'll do something awful. I don't know what yet, but I will.'

Munro opened his mouth and closed it again without speaking. After a few seconds, he said, 'Will you be at home this evening, Keith?'

'I expect so. Why?'

'A body has been found, cause of death so far undetermined.' He twisted to look behind him. Deborah's face, usually carefree and delicately pink, was an almost luminous white. 'No,' he said quickly, 'it is not the Sergeant. And it was found in the Forth. It might be Robert Hall. If no other identification turns up shortly, they may be inviting you to go and identify it.'

'Just what I needed to round off a perfect day,' Keith said. 'What happened to the van?'

'I believe that it has been towed away.'

'Tell them to take good care of it. I'm responsible. Also it has some of my things in it.'

When the Chief Superintendent had disentangled himself and left them, Deborah climbed over into the passenger seat. 'Dad!' she said reproachfully. 'How could you? Ian may be in the most awful trouble and all you can think of is the things you lent him.'

Keith drove off, out of the town and along the road towards home. 'That isn't all I'm thinking about,' he said. 'But we don't know that Ian's in any bother and I don't see that he'd be helped by my forgetting about a good pair of binoculars.'

'Well, I think we should be doing something.'

'So do I. But what?'

'I don't know,' Deborah said miserably.

'Nor do I. When I do know, we'll do it. Meantime, I know what I've got to do and that's to find somebody else to take on Robert Hall's job.'

'Dad, you're heartless!'

Keith had never felt less like laughing but he managed

to force a chuckle. 'Remind me of that, next time you want a favour,' he said.

An elegant upstairs room in a spacious old house in Broughty Ferry was doing duty as a command post. Usually a haven of peace, it was pulsing with the nervous energy of its occupants.

The room had been furnished for a professional man who liked to work in comfort and from home. There was a sumptuous swivel chair at a large and highly polished mahogany desk. Several leather-covered easy-chairs were centred around the Adam fireplace. The carpet was deep and the paintings on the panelled walls were original, chosen as much for capital appreciation as for beauty. Papers were usually confined to the matching bookcases or banished to the starker room next door which had once been reserved for the use of a visiting secretary.

At the desk, which was set at a bay window and in clearer weather commanded a view over the yacht club to Tayport, one telephone was in use and a light on the other indicated that the extension in the adjoining room was also being used.

In front of the unlit fire, the thickset American stood as if to heat his behind with the residual warmth of flames long dead. His hands, deep in his pockets, were gently massaging away the pain. Dora Braddle, slumped like a sack of suet in one of the deep armchairs, glared at the ceiling.

Charles Hanratty, the owner of the house, was seated at the large corner-table usually reserved for the study of his collection of oriental erotica. The table was now spread with charts and littered with instruments. He was a tall, silver-haired man blessed with aloof poise. His manner towards the others was superior, even patronising. That he was vain was evident from his manicured fingernails, the careful removal of hair from his ears and nostrils and an opulent dapperness in his clothes.

59

'So much for the Fife coast,' Hanratty said. He adjusted a pair of heavily framed spectacles on his Roman nose. 'Now we should look further afield.'

'How far could they go?' Dora asked.

'It's been four hours now. Given a decent breeze they could be past Arbroath going north, or entering the Forth if they went south. Further, if they risked the Cut. They could make Aberdeen in twelve hours or get down as far as the Tyne in about eighteen.'

'But there isn't any breeze,' Dora Braddle pointed out.

'There isn't any breeze here,' said Hanratty. 'But here is where they are not. The forecast mentioned a shallow depression to the south. That could give them a nice little onshore breeze which hasn't got here yet. And *Lonely Lady* sails well on a reach. I've raced against her.'

'Never mind the crap,' Dora said. 'Just tell us where to put men.'

The man at the phone finished his call. Hanratty looked at him and glanced at Dora. She nodded. 'Directory Enquiries, Foxy,' Hanratty said. 'You want the Forth Ports Authority. They can give us the numbers for Granton, Leith, North Berwick and Dunbar. And while you've got Enquiries, get the numbers for the marinas at the Queensferries.'

'I've got contacts at North Berwick,' Dora said.

'Get Mike to phone them on the other line. We want Aberlady and Tyninghame Bays covered and a watch kept from the road out to St Abb's Head.'

'I'll fix it,' Dora said. 'Anywhere else?'

'Does your man in Pittenweem still have a lobster boat available for . . . special tasks?'

Dora twitched in her chair. Hanratty was not supposed to know that her agent was available, for a fee, to convey unwanted objects or inconvenient memories into deep water and there to lose them for ever. 'Yes,' she said.

'Send him out to May Island. The shore station has a

60

radio-phone but they wouldn't pass private messages for us over the air to the lighthousekeepers. On the other hand, the lighthouse staff might be persuaded to radio a message to the police in an emergency. Tell your man to wait in the anchorage at West Tarbert. They'd be mad to use Kirkhaven with the wind in the east.'

'I'll deal with it from the other room,' Dora said. She pushed herself to her feet, exchanging eye-signals with the American.

Hanratty failed to notice the small exchange. 'Now for the north,' he said. 'That skipper may have mistaken some other boat for *Lonely Lady*. We'd better cover the coast as far as Peterhead.' He lost himself in his charts.

The American muttered something about the bathroom. Dora beckoned through the open door. Foxy, at the telephone, looked up but she shook her head at him. The American walked casually out and pulled the door to. Dora led him along the corridor until they were well out of earshot.

'If those two don't fall into our hands soon,' she said, 'we've got problems.'

He nodded sombrely. 'There'll be a chain reaction. But the problem's all yours. I got what I came for and I can go back into the shadows. It was mostly to save your ass that I grabbed the woman in the first place. The only reason I've stuck around as long as I have is that I want to see that bugger put down, the one who smacked me in the passionfruits.'

'If you hadn't grabbed her,' Dora said bitterly, 'we wouldn't be in this fix. She'd never have known what she'd got. And I wouldn't have been stamped on.' She rubbed her round stomach reflectively.

'In the end, the shit always floats to the surface. When there's been a big hit, they dig and dig until they've got the lot. If it isn't the cops it's the writers trying to prove a theory.'

'Is your target that big? No, don't tell me,' she added quickly.

'I wasn't going to.'

'If we go,' Dora said, 'I leave first.'

'Of course,' the American said. Behind his smile, his mind was ticking over smoothly. If Dora was so anxious to make off with the money he had just paid her, it must mean that she expected Mary Bruce to freeze Dora's share of their joint capital as soon as it was known that the latter had drawn unwelcome attention to their activities. Sharks, he knew, would turn and rend a wounded companion, but sharks were as innocent lambs compared to those ladies. 'If you do a bunk, I suppose Mary Bruce carries the can?'

'With luck.' Dora shrugged. 'It's a tough old world,' she said.

'Her dad won't be pleased.'

'Her dad won't be around for another year and then he'd have to find me.'

'What about . . . ?' The American pointed towards the closed door.

Dora drew her finger across her throat. Her smile redeemed her sharp features. For a moment she was almost beautiful.

'Couldn't be better,' the man said.

May Island stands in the mouth of the Firth of Forth, five miles from either shore. Afternoon wore on towards evening as they held course towards the island. They ate tinned steak and drank milkless tea. Sheila would have sold her soul for one dry cigarette. To distract herself from what she knew to be an unworthy craving, she offered only token resistance when Ian invited her to talk about herself.

Being pitchforked from a humdrum existence into adventure had left Sheila without any sense of reality. She might have been fumbling for recollection of some previous incarnation. And yet it all came across. Ian could picture it clearly. The childhood in Forfar, doting on a father who left control and discipline to her mother. The shock of her father's death. Inevitable friction with her mother, by now too domineering to relent. Secretarial college and a dull but independent job. The engagement which failed because of the need to support and nurse an ailing mother. Hostility suppressed, replaced by guilt.

Then, dreaded yet welcome, freedom and a small legacy, sufficient to buy a studio flat and to aim herself at her real ambition. She talked about the routine at Duncan of Jordanstone College of Art, and Ian could sense more than she told him. Her face and her tone said more than her words. Freedom had arrived too late. She was enthralled by her work but disappointed that her classmates, finding her older than themselves and mistaking her shyness for reserve, had gently but firmly excluded her from their corporate liveliness. She would have liked her studio to be a salon but it was becoming a prison. She knew that they were calling her 'Chill' Blayne behind her back, but she withheld that detail from him.

She came back to the present when the wind backed and *Lonely Lady* began to roll.

They could have had it rough off Fife Ness, where the tide makes its turn over a shelving bottom, but rather than risk being seen from the shore Ian had set a course which took them past well out to sea. The breeze returned to the east, bringing only a long swell to which *Lonely Lady* lifted gracefully.

The mist was still there, usually little more than a haze but thickening in random patches as the day cooled. Once it blew clear so that the coast of Fife showed up and Sheila could feel hostile eyes on her, but Ian calmed her fears, explaining how inconspicuous was a small boat with tan sails at such a distance. The breeze fell light and the mist closed in again. They began to hear the lowing of the two foghorns on May Island.

63

Ian gave Sheila the helm. He set a new course on the compass and freed the sails for what was now nearer to a run than a reach. He got to his feet – stiffly, after sitting for so long – and stood on the side-deck, one arm around a shroud, feeding the coils of the hand-line from hand to hand. The mist was thicker around the island.

'I'll be watching for rocks and feeling for the bottom at seven fathoms,' he said. 'When I make anxious noises, act quickly. Push the tiller the way I point. Never mind what the sails do, I'll sort them out later; just let's not sail onto the rocks.' He gripped the line above a tag of red bunting, swung the lead and let the line shoot ahead. As it came vertical, he felt for the bottom. 'Nothing yet,' he said. He paused in the act of coiling the wet line. 'I wonder why they set up their meet at Broughty Ferry, of all places.'

Sheila brooded anxiously over the grid compass, reminding herself again that the card moved in the same direction as the tiller and not the other way as she would have expected. 'It had to be somewhere,' she said.

'But why there? If he's American and she's Glasgow.'

'The gun was made in Dundee.'

'So meet in Dundee or somewhere further south and west, not Broughty. It would be against her instincts to travel in the opposite direction from home, when what she was carrying could land her in the deepest trouble of her life.' He finished coiling the line and cast it again. The nearer foghorn boomed, eerily, slightly muted as if land were beginning to obtrude between it and them.

'If it means anything,' Sheila said, 'I'd seen Dora Braddle once before. I saw her earlier in the day from the bus. She was going into one of those big houses across the main road from the yacht club.'

Ian was coiling the line again. It dribbled cold water onto his bare feet and he moaned softly. 'That could explain it,' he said. 'If the money was lying in the hands of a minder, a third party . . . '

'Yes, but listen,' Sheila said. 'The reason I noticed her at all was that I knew the house. A girl in my year used to live there. She dropped out to get married. Joan Hanratty. I was at the wedding.'

Ian waited while his line sank. He felt for the bottom and found it. At the same moment, rocks showed out of the mist. Sheila squeaked and put the helm over. Ian dropped into the cockpit and took it from her, steering with his knee while he tried to recover the hand-line and adjust the sheets. 'Hanratty?' he said. 'Hanratty? What does her father do?'

'I think he was something to do with the law, but he seems to be retired now. I met him at her wedding. I didn't like him much. He seemed to be too proud of his possessions. People who take too much pride in owning things never seem to have anything in themselves to be proud of. And he was vain about his youthfulness,' she added. 'You know the type. A solarium for a tan and his hearing-aid hidden in his spectacle frames.'

'Jesus!' Ian put the helm further over and sheered away from the island. The sails slatted. He sheeted in and they were away on a reach to the south again. The rocks faded into the mist and the foghorns called plaintively after them. 'There was a solicitor named Hanratty. He got struck off last year. I always read up these cases, partly out of professional interest and partly in a spirit of "There but for the grace of God go the rest of them". No other profession finds dishonesty so easy, or so tempting. He'd been up to several fiddles, mostly in connection with wills and conveyances – which makes him sound like perfect legal help for Dora. Listen, tell me, before we even think about going near land again, did he sail?'

Sheila thought back. 'Yes,' she said at last. 'I remember Joan saying something about money being tight and her father having to give up his boat.'

'Thank God for talkative friends!' Ian said grimly. 'If they've got a sailor on the team, he won't forget

May Island. We'll go on south. They've got to let up somewhere.'

'Maybe they let up at the Tay.'

'Maybe. But suddenly I've taken a scunner to May Island. And to Dunbar. What kind of boat did he have? Dinghy? Day-sailor? Gin-palace? Ocean-racer?'

'I know that they could sleep ‾on board,' Sheila said helplessly. 'I never knew her all that well and she only spoke about it the once. She mentioned Elie and Aberdour.'

'That does it!' said Ian. 'We go round the corner and continue south. I don't fancy St Abb's or Eyemouth, they're too small and too close; and I wouldn't fancy Burnmouth in an onshore wind and in the dark even if nobody were after us. I think we'll try Berwick-on-Tweed. Two large towns facing each other, a wide harbour-mouth and a choice of docks. I think we'll take a look at the Tweed in the early morning.'

'Whatever you say.'

'Are you tired?'

'Not particularly.'

'Well, I'm pooped.' Ian yawned vastly at the thought. 'I don't think I slept for more than an hour last night, in an armchair in the van. You take over while I have a doze. This course should clear St Abb's Head. You'll see the light flashing every ten seconds away to starboard – that side,' he explained carefully. 'Anything else, bang on the deck and scream bloody murder. Wear my watch. Wake me at three if I'm still sleeping or earlier if you feel yourself beginning to doze off. Got it?'

'I think so,' Sheila said.

'You can see a lighthouse flashing, even without your glasses?'

'Don't be silly!' she said.

At first, Charles Hanratty had found the planning of the hunt intellectually stimulating. His enjoyment of a contest of the mind had been his pleasure in legal practice and the motivation which had tempted him away from its strict precepts. And it was a boost to his ego to know that a group of such strong personalities depended on him for his expertise.

But, when the evening sun began to glow flatly through the clearing mist, the atmosphere in the room had changed from expectation to despondency and his mood had changed with it. He resented the imperious despatch of his wife to stay with their married daughter and the commandeering of his house and services; and he was uncomfortably aware that he had already lost his licence to practise as a solicitor and was in great danger of losing also his less legal but equally profitable connections. Worst of all, he now knew too much.

He had decided some hours earlier that his salvation lay in a successful outcome to the chase. He might not like his horse but he must ride it to win. For the moment. If it fell or came second, then he would know that it was possible to outrun Dora's long arm. His instinct told him it was being nosed out.

Dora finished her call and hung up the phone. 'Nothing,' she said. 'They could have gone to the moon.'

The American stirred in one of the armchairs. 'If your man Grotty says that nobody's been near your place,' he said, 'then as of half an hour ago our two young friends haven't made contact with the police.'

'Unless there's been a trap set,' Dora said. 'I can't get an answer on Mary's line. I don't like it a bit. Could those two be holed up somewhere?'

'That's possible,' Hanratty said. 'There are drilling rigs laid up near the coast and small bays and anchorages which would be safe in this weather. If that's what they've done, it becomes a waiting game. My bet is that they've pushed on south. Do you have any hard men in Northumberland?'

'Tweedmouth's covered,' Dora said.

'I'm thinking of Holy Island. Do you have anyone in Newcastle or Blyth?'

'That's off my patch,' Dora said. 'Grotty knows a man in Seahouses, but we've already sent him out with his boat. I could get somebody down from Glasgow before that yacht could get there.'

Hanratty glanced from his watch to the tide tables. 'Tell him to get his skates on or he'll not get over the causeway at low tide.'

'I'll phone from next door and keep this line free for incoming calls,' Dora said. She looked at Hanratty with cold eyes. 'I don't like what you said about a waiting game. We can't afford it. If those two sailed to an oil rig, would the staff radio the police?'

'That's for sure,' the American said.

Dora had not taken her eyes off Hanratty. 'Or they could speak to some other yacht. While we wait, the law could be preparing to pounce. We need those two sods and we need them soon. That's your job.'

'And I'm doing all that's humanly possible,' Hanratty said. 'I can't make things move any faster just to get you off my back. If I could, believe me, I would.'

Dora barely caught the American's eye as she left the room but he joined her as she finished her Glasgow call. Her handbag, of alligator skin to match her shoes, was open on the desk.

'I don't go for this,' he said. 'Every minute that goes by stretches the mesh of the net wider.'

'And involves more men at a hundred a day each,' Dora said grimly. 'Plus the bounty, if one of them hits the bull's-eye. Christ! I might save more than I lost by skipping out right away. I think . . . yes, I think we've got to distance ourselves from this little operation. We'll let it run on but I'll monitor it from a distance. Grotty can start tidying up. He'll know soon enough if those two have made it to the authorities, and if that happens he cleans out my bank account and waits for me in London.'

'You'd trust a man called Grotty?' the American asked incredulously.

Dora smiled bleakly. 'I've got enough on Grotty to send him away for a thousand years after remission. Of course I trust him. I wouldn't send him out to rob a piggy bank, he's not the active type. But as a background man, he's good.'

Without speaking, the American flicked his eyes towards the room next door.

Dora smiled. 'Dear Charles,' she said, heaving herself to her feet. 'He may have outlived his usefulness. But, for the moment, we need his services. Mike and Foxy can keep him here and put him down if the worst comes to the worst. But I'll tell you this, his prospects aren't good.' She turned back from the door to collect her handbag.

In the large room, Mike and Foxy were playing a game with matches. There was no sign of Hanratty.

'Where's he gone?' Dora asked.

'To the crapper, he said.'

'Its door was open,' said the American, 'but we didn't hear it flush. He's run for it.'

Outside, an engine started. The car moved away in a hurry.

'I can catch him,' the American said. He raced down the stairs, pretending not to hear Dora calling after him. Outside the front door, he threw himself into his own car; but when he had the engine running he did not go after Hanratty. Instead, he headed for where he had left his caravan. The modified rifle was safely locked in the boot of his car. By the time Dora discovered that the money he had paid her was missing, the car would have been replaced, the caravan dumped and his appearance subtly changed. If Mary Bruce froze her other assets, the word would soon go around that Dora could not afford to pay for information.

Old favours are no substitute for new currency.

Lonely Lady lost time during the night. The breeze had fallen away to light airs and Ian had decided to reserve that last inch of petrol in the outboard's tank for emergencies.

It was mid-morning before he lowered the mainsail, hooked the main halliard to a rope knotted into the approximate form of a bosun's chair and made his third trip up the mast. The reviving breeze, which had cleared the mist away at last, pressed the big genoa and held the boat steady enough to let him use the rusty but efficient binoculars which her owner had left aboard *Lonely Lady*.

His first visit to the masthead had shown that his dead reckoning was out and that they were still opposite Burnmouth. On his second attempt he had seen the buildings of Berwick, the high bridge over the Tweed and even the clock on the Town Hall, but the harbour-mouth had still been below the horizon. But now he could see the small lighthouse on the end of the pier. He waited for the boat's motion to steady and took a long look through the binoculars.

He let himself down the mast in a hurry. 'Come round to the south again,' he said.

'We aren't going in?'

'Not in there,' he said. 'Not this trip.'

'I'm hungry,' Sheila said plaintively.

'So am I. But there's a van parked right at the pier-end. We'd have to pass close by it or risk going on the sand at Spittal Point. It may be quite innocent. It may belong to a fisherman or to somebody maintaining the lighthouse. On the other hand, one of Dora's friends may be sitting in it with a rifle. You want to take a chance on it? Or shall we go on to Holy Island?'

Sheila weighed her hunger against her fear. Fear won. 'How far is Holy Island?' she asked.

'About two hours, with luck.' Ian spoke from the foot of the mast where he was re-setting the mainsail. 'By my reckoning the causeway will be covered soon. I'd like to get in and out before it uncovers again.' He glanced at Sheila and, seeing her incomprehension, took pity. 'The reason I fancy Holy Island is that, weather permitting and if your keel isn't too deep, you can get in and out by boat at any time; but you can only get over from the mainland by car or on foot when the tide's down. It's not much of an advantage but at least we can shade the odds in our favour. With a bit of luck, if they sent somebody he missed the tide. Or if they have somebody there, the knowledge that he can't get off for a few hours may cramp his style.'

Sheila was tired and her face was burning from the salt and sun. The whole trip was beginning to resemble a dream in which she kept struggling on and on, only to find that Journey's End came no closer. 'From Holy Island, do we go home?'

'We think about it.'

'I'm already thinking about it,' she said sadly. 'Do people really do this sort of thing for fun?'

Five

In Glasgow, Grotty stopped feeding papers through the shredder to answer the telephone.

Nicknames are often humorously inappropriate, but whoever had first given Grotty his soubriquet had found the *mot juste*. He was ugly, dirty and scruffy and his breath smelled. In the severely functional study of Dora's austere flat, he looked as out of place as a cowpat in a dairy. But he was loyal and he would have been loyal to Dora even if she had not had a vice-like hold over him.

Grotty's loyalty to Dora sprang from admiration rather than affection. He admired her ruthless courage. Grotty himself could be ruthless at a distance, although he lacked the nerve for direct action. But, as Dora had said, he was an efficient organiser and she had given up trying to remedy his failings.

'Aye, lass,' Grotty said into the phone. 'I'll accept the charges.' He glanced up at the wall, where a large map was copiously annotated in black felt-tip.

'Go ahead, caller.'

'Dora? You there, hen?'

'This is Grotty.'

'Jimmy Jay here, Grotty.'

'Chrissake, Jimmy, I bloody know it's you. How could I no', with you reversing the charges? What in hell you doing at Beal? You're supposed to be on the island.'

'Got me car drowned, didn't I? First it was fog an'

then I picked up a nail, bloody miles from anywhere. An' then my spare was flat.'

'You stupid sod!' Grotty said.

'But it was your mate Foxy used my car last. He must've had a puncture an' not said.' Jimmy Jay's voice, already plaintive, came close to tears. 'So there I was, not a soul around or even a light to be seen. I walked miles an' miles until I found a filling station. All locked up, of course, an' no bugger around except a couple of Alsatians just waiting the chance to chew my balls off. I'd to wait until the feller turned up, an' then twist his arm before he'd help. Then we got back to my car. Still no bugger for miles around, but hadn't somebody pinched my battery?'

Grotty deferred telling him to come to the point. He was enjoying the story. 'Go on,' he said.

'He wouldn't take a cheque, not after the way I'd gone on at him, an' by the time I'd paid for the tow an' the punctures an' some petrol I couldn't pay for a new battery.'

'You could've duffed him up and taken one,' Grotty suggested.

'Not when I'd got to hang around just a few miles off I couldn't,' Jimmy Jay said reasonably. 'He fixed me up with a second-hander that'd done a million miles an' gave me a jump-lead start, but by the time I got here the causeway was just being covered an' the tide coming up fast. I tried it anyway, but the car drowned an' I waded back to shore. I don't reckon I can get on to the island for another couple of hours. Even then, I'll have to walk across. Unless you want me to hitch into Seahouses an' steal a boat?'

Grotty consulted his map and sighed. There was a breach in the defences and no way to seal it. Even now, the phone-lines from Holy Island might be humming. 'That'd take you longer,' he said, 'and while you're farting around off the Farne Islands they go ashore over the causeway. You did save your shooter from the car?'

'Surely. Will Dora pay for the car, do you think?'

'You'll be lucky, fucking it up like this. Listen. It's locking the stable door, but you go and watch the end of the causeway. If those two come ashore – a red-haired bloke in his thirties, built like he's played rugby, and a stringy bird, around the same age, light brown hair, brown eyes and a figure like a lamppost with knockers – you deal with them. If they don't come after the causeway uncovers, you go out to the island. They won't be there, but you can find out if they've been. Phone me.'

'Not my fault, running over a nail. An' if I waste them both, how do I get away with no car?'

'That's your problem,' Grotty said, 'and you'd better have an answer. Or do you want to look over your shoulder some day and see Dora behind you, smiling?' If those two slipped through, Grotty thought to himself, Dora would be too busy to exact petty revenges, but there was no point just yet in laying down the stick.

Jimmy Jay's sudden shiver came audibly over the wire.

In Briesland House near Newton Lauder, Keith was at his workbench. He was making poor progress with the restoration of the German wheel-lock which he wanted to prepare for inclusion in his forthcoming catalogue. His every attempt to resume work was foiled by a fresh outburst from Deborah.

'Dad,' she said for the umpteenth time, 'you've got to phone Mr Munro.'

Keith was as anxious as his daughter, but he was more capable of taking a realistic view. 'He'll let us know as soon as there's any news,' he said.

'But he won't *do* anything. And Ian may be in some awful danger. He may be in desperate need of help.'

'Not much Munro can do until something happens,' Keith said.

'But he's police,' Deborah said, as though that endowed

74

the Chief Superintendent with magical powers. 'He can spread the word, have people watching, all that sort of thing,' she finished lamely.

'You phone him.'

'He treats me as though I was still twelve years old.'

Keith knew only too well that any precipitate action by Munro before Sergeant Fellowes surfaced, preferably in possession of valuable evidence, would put the Chief Superintendent in the untenable position of admitting that he had sent a subordinate, who was not one of his own team, into possible danger without any help or back-up. But Keith had never been able to withstand sustained nagging by either of his womenfolk. With a last, sad glance at the wheel-lock he spun his stool around and picked up the phone.

Chief Superintendent Munro picked up his extension phone on the first ring. When he recognised Keith's voice, the hope in his own died away. 'No,' he said. 'No news yet.'

'We're very anxious,' Keith said. 'More than anxious. Frantic would better describe one or two of us.'

'And you think that I am not . . . frantic? I have never been so worried.'

'It's been more than twenty-four hours now,' Keith said. 'Worrying isn't enough any more. I know how you're placed and I sympathise; but while you play it close to your chest some bobby may be in a position to give Sergeant Fellowes the help which might save his neck, but doesn't know it. You've got to warn all forces.'

Deborah put her cheek against her father's. 'If you don't,' she said, 'I'm going to the newspapers.'

Keith pushed her away. There was a stunned silence at the other end. 'Keith?' said Munro's voice at last.

'Yes?'

'For the love of God do not let her do any such thing. What you were saying is just what I have been

75

telling myself, but I have been putting off admitting my sins.'

'I understand all that. If you can produce Ian Fellowes, complete with evidence that your *bête noire* McHarg refused to act on information about a planned assassination – information which turns out to be valid – you'll be the hero of the hour and McHarg the villain, whereas—'

'Do not even say it aloud,' Munro begged. 'It is all just as you say, but I could not stand hearing the words. Give me just a little longer.'

'How little?'

'The morn's morn?' Munro asked hopefully.

'Too late.'

'Until midnight, then?'

Keith avoided his daughter's eye. 'If there's no word from Ian Fellowes by midnight, you'll set all the wheels in motion? All of them?'

There was another hiatus while Munro wrestled with himself. 'I promise,' he said at last. 'And you'll keep the lassie away from the media?'

'If you keep your word. In fact, there's no question of her ringing the press.'

'I am relieved to hear it.'

'Because,' Keith said firmly, 'it would be very much more effective if she just phoned Superintendent McHarg.'

He hung up on the Chief Superintendent's indignant squawk.

'But, Dad,' Deborah said, 'something could happen to Ian between now and midnight.'

Keith could not deny it. Nor dared he point out that if Sergeant Fellowes was destined to meet terminal trouble he had probably already done so. With relief, he heard the sound of the front doorbell.

'Is your mother home yet?'

'No.'

76

'See who that is.'

'Shall I send him away?' Deborah asked. 'Unless it's a customer, of course.'

'Bring him up, whoever it is,' Keith said. Any interruption would be better than being forced to take a share in Deborah's agonising.

He gained a minute or two in which to drill holes in the chain-links which he was fabricating for the wheel-lock. Then he heard the sound of two sets of footsteps on the stairs.

Deborah arrived in the doorway. 'It's a Mr Cardinal,' she said.

'Paul Cardinal,' said the newcomer. 'Call me Paul.' He was a large man, tall and barrel-chested. Greying hair was cropped close on his round head. His face was keen but otherwise expressionless. His clothes were for leisure but they were spotless, of good quality and nearly new. He glanced around the big room, which had been made by throwing together two large bedrooms, and his eyes widened as they took in the neat racks of antique guns. 'Hey, this is some den you've gotten here!'

Keith pulled out the visitor's chair for him and resumed the stool. Deborah hopped up onto the end of the workbench.

'Ah, come on!' Cardinal said. 'Let the young lady have the chair. I'm tall enough, I can sit on the bench and stand, both.'

'Not in those trousers, you can't,' Deborah said more cheerfully. The small courtesy had eased her tense mood. 'My jeans won't take any harm.'

'She seldom sits anywhere else,' Keith said.

Paul Cardinal shrugged, produced a hint of a smile and sat. 'I was recommended to come to you,' he said.

The faint, American accent jogged Keith's memory. 'I think you spoke with Chief Superintendent Munro,' he said.

77

Cardinal's impassive face lengthened in surprise. 'That's right,' he said.

'I assume that his recommendation didn't bring you here?'

'He told me that you don't get to carry a side-arm over here for self-defence.'

'He was telling the truth,' Keith said. (He almost added 'for once'.) 'They think that the total number of deaths comes out lower that way. Of course, it may be the wrong people who get killed, but the statistics look better. Mr Cardinal—'

'I'm not used to that mode of address. Call me Paul. Please.'

'Very well. But first name terms still won't persuade me to sell you an off-register hand-gun. You'll find one easily enough if you ask around in the rougher bars. Of course, there's nothing to hinder you from buying an antique pistol. You'd be breaking the law if you loaded it, of course, but I wouldn't know about that.'

'It's a thought. But I can look after myself, with or without a pistol. That isn't at all what I came to see you about. Somebody at the hotel told me that you know everybody in these parts and all the local history.'

'I wouldn't put it like that,' Keith said. 'I know a lot of people. And you can't make a lifelong study of weapons without picking up some of the history that goes with them.'

'What Dad means,' Deborah said, 'is that he's read every book in the world about old wars and things.'

'You flatter me,' Keith said.

Paul Cardinal was nodding. 'That's the sort of history I'm looking for. I'd better tell you the story, if you can spare me the time.'

Keith glanced at Deborah. 'We have time to fill,' he said.

Paul Cardinal looked at the unfinished work on the

bench but made no comment. 'I retired kind of early,' he said. 'I was a detective with LAPD. Los Angeles, you know?'

'Like Colombo?' Deborah said.

'Yep. Only it was never just like that. I enjoyed the work, but there's no denying it's a three-ulcer job on a two-ulcer salary. Then, a few years back, I could afford to get out; so I thought what the hell? No, I wasn't taking graft,' Paul added quickly, recognising an expression which Keith had been slow to mask. 'I had a big win on LOTTO – that's the California State Lottery. You pick six two-figure numbers. It can pay out big bucks.'

'Big enough to retire on?' Keith asked doubtfully.

'If nobody's guessed all the numbers and the main prize isn't won, it gets rolled over to swell the jackpot for next time. The biggest win so far was sixty-two million dollars, split three ways.'

'I'm almost afraid to ask—' Deborah began.

'Mine wasn't quite that big and it was split between five, but it was big. I didn't retire right away. I've always enjoyed a gamble, so I used the money to back inventions. Three times a hunk of money went down the drain. Then we hit the jackpot again with a new-type all-weather tennis court. It's a good product but I guess our slogan helped – "Play in the rain without getting your balls wet". I came out with twice my original win.

'A gambler I may be, but putting my life on the line several times a week for a monthly wage was getting to seem like poor odds, so I got out.

'My mother was an Elliot and her folks came from hereabouts. I'd spent some time in Europe and I thought I'd like to find out more about my ancestry over here. To start with, I employed professionals. It cost but it was great value. They traced the family back and back until they came to a "Laird's Tam Elliot" who was one of the Border reivers. He was hanged at Carlisle Castle in seventeen thirty-five.'

79

'I've got bad news for you already,' Keith said. 'If that's the right date, he wasn't a reiver. That period ended with the Act of Union and the Pacification when Scotland took over England.' Both his listeners looked blank. 'It was a Scottish king who gained the English crown, not the other way around. I'm afraid your ancestor, Laird's Tam, was just a bad hat.'

'I can believe it,' Paul said. 'I nearly gave up just then. I could do without a gangster in the family. But what they told me tied up with a letter that'd been in my mother's family since the year nothing, almost. The original's locked away in a safe-deposit, but I have a photocopy here.'

From an inside pocket of his golf-jacket, Paul produced a folded paper and handed it to Keith. Deborah hopped down and stooped to look over her father's shoulder.

The photocopy was of an original which seemed to be faded, creased and stained, but the ill-formed words painstakingly written could still be made out.

Carlyl
Jan'y

Katherin, dear wyf,
It seems we'll no be trystin mair. Kiss the laddies for me and tell them they was in my thochts.

We had sair need of ane of the weedae McLean's yows. She's a puir body. Ax Aikhowe can he repone. Gie him this Guid Book. There's monie a muckle truth hid in its pages.

My yae efterstang's that I'll no be hame to mynd yersel an the loons. Be suir o my love to the end.

Aye your Tam

'It's sad,' Deborah whispered.

Keith's reaction was more mundane. 'The wording looks about right,' he said. 'Without seeing the original, it's difficult to be sure.'

'It's genuine, right enough,' Paul Cardinal said. 'My grandmother showed it to me when I was just a kid.'

'She told you what it means?'

'I guess so. Family legend was that he wrote it from his death-bed, but I guess it was from the condemned cell, if they had such a place. He's saying goodbye to his wife and kids. And he sent his Bible to this Aikhowe, whoever he was.'

'There weren't enough names to go round,' Keith said. 'Nicknames were commonly used and chieftains were often known by the names of their houses. Laird's Tam was probably Aikhowe's son, legitimate or otherwise.'

While he spoke, Keith was still regarding the photocopy, his forehead creased in doubt. On top of two disappearances, the sudden arrival of a stranger with an improbable tale to tell merited caution.

They heard the sound of the front door closing. He looked at Deborah. 'Pop downstairs,' he said. 'Warn your mum that there may be another for dinner. And bring me up the correspondence file from the study.'

'Don't take it too far before I get back,' she said. 'This is getting interesting.' To her father's pleasure, she was recovering a little of her animation.

'Now,' Keith said as the door closed, 'let's just do a little checking. You were with the Los Angeles Police Department?'

'That's right.'

'Did you know anybody in the Sheriff's Department?'

'One or two. Where's this going?'

'James Hochmeier?'

'Sure. Knew him well.'

'He wrote to me last month. He'd picked up a "Rotary" model Darne from near the end of the nineteenth century. He wanted to know more about the history. He introduced himself as being with the Los Angeles Sheriff.'

Deborah returned. 'Was that just a ploy to get me out of the room or is this what you want?' She put down the file, open, in front of her father.

Paul Cardinal pointed a finger at Keith. 'You think this is a con,' he said.

'I don't think anything. But it has the makings.'

'Damned if it doesn't!' Cardinal sounded surprised.

'So do you mind if I phone Detective Hochmeier?'

'He's a sergeant, but go right ahead.' Cardinal glanced at a thin wrist-watch. 'He'll have left for work by now. I can give you the Sheriff's number.'

'Jot it down for me.'

Cardinal wrote down a code and number from memory but Keith dialled the number at the head of the letter. Far away in California, Mrs Hochmeier answered the phone in a sleepy drawl. Her husband would be at the Sheriff's office by now. She gave him the number. It agreed with the one that Paul Cardinal had written on Keith's scratch-pad.

Keith dialled again and the Los Angeles Sheriff's Department came on the line. Sergent Hochmeier, it seemed, was out.

'When will he be back?'

'Where are you calling from?' asked the distant voice.

'Scotland.'

'Jeepers! Hold the line. I'll patch you through to his car.'

'Thank you,' Keith said. He was impressed.

'No trouble.'

Another voice came on the line. Keith introduced himself. Sergeant Hochmeier was delighted to hear from him. 'Say, Mr Calder, the material you sent me about that Darne just cast up a day or two back.'

'Was it what you wanted?'

'Right on the button. Hold on while I pull over. Say, I was going to write back and thank you but I put it off while I wondered what I could do in return.'

82

'Now's your chance,' Keith said. 'Did you know a Paul Cardinal with LAPD?'

'Sure I knew him,' Hochmeier said. 'We were together on the Anti-terrorist Task Force for around three years.'

Keith handed over the receiver. 'Hello there, Jimbo,' Cardinal said. 'How's Rena? And do you still pass blood?'

He took the receiver away from his ear so that Keith could hear the reply. 'Rena's fine. And I got the piles fixed. No my ass only hurts when I think of you.'

'Likewise,' Cardinal said. He handed the phone back to Keith.

'That was Paul Cardinal?'

'That was Paul,' Hochmeier confirmed. 'Whatever he is, there's only one of it; and that was the original. What's he doing over there in Scotland?'

'I'm just finding out. Thanks for the help. I just wanted to be sure.'

'Think nothing of it. You went to some trouble, looking out all that material on the "Rotary" Darne. Is there anything else I can do for you?'

'You could take a couple of tickets in the LOTTO for me,' Keith said.

'Sure. I'll do that. What numbers?'

'You've got my phone-number and code there. Use that.'

When the call was finished, Keith hung up. 'So you're Paul Cardinal, ex-LAPD,' he said. 'Is that why you wanted a pistol?'

'Sure. After I left the Anti-terrorist Task Force I was on secondment over here for a while. No problem carrying a hand-gun then.' He spared a sigh for the good old days. 'I've put away some professional hit-men in my time. Some of those guys can bear a grudge – they don't have much else to think about in the pen. I don't think anyone's looking for me, here and now, but I haven't lived this long by being careless.'

83

'You interest us more and more,' Keith said. 'You'll stay to dinner?'

While Deborah, in deference to one of the few inflexible rules in the Calder household, changed into a frock for the evening meal, Keith had a few words with Paul Cardinal.

'Deborah's fiancé is in the police,' he said. 'Another detective sergeant. He was on an observation job and he hasn't reported in. She's worried sick – we all are. If the subject comes up . . . '

'Soft pedal?'

'Right,' Keith said. 'Help me try to keep her mind occupied. It doesn't look good, but there's no point saying so until we know.'

Paul Cardinal nodded soberly. 'I got you. Faced the same thing a dozen times. Once or twice it came out all right. Hope this is one of them.'

'So do we all,' Keith said. 'Let's try to keep talking about other things. Come and have a drink.'

'You're sure that I won't be in the way, at such a time?'

'You'll be a valuable distraction.'

Molly Calder dearly loved entertaining guests, even last-minute additions to the table. Some clever work with the microwave oven stretched the meat to four servings and they sat down to a good meal. Keith had brought two books to the table – usually an unforgivable sin but Molly, appeased by the good manners of the guest, decided to overlook the offending books as long as they lay unopened beside Keith. To keep the talk away from the subject of Ian Fellowes, Keith encouraged Paul Cardinal to regale Molly with the story of his luckless ancestor.

Deborah knew the workings of her father's mind. She put aside her anxiety and asked him, 'Dad, what was wrong with the letter?'

'Good question,' Paul said. 'What made you think that I might be setting you up?'

Molly tutted. 'I'm sure that he thought no such thing.'

'I did, in fact. Thinking it over now,' Keith said, 'I can see explanations that make sense. But my first reaction was two-fold. Those were rough days. But the day of the reivers was past. The reivers were driven to their lawlessness by the need to survive. They managed to retain at least some codes of morality. After the Pacification, those codes lapsed. I just couldn't see how a man facing the gallows would worry about a widow's sheep. That's what a yow is,' he added.

Paul nodded. 'A ewe,' he said.

'Right. Nor could I see him taking a Bible with him on a foray.'

'He might have been given one, after he was sentenced,' Molly said.

'That's very likely what happened,' Keith said. 'But why would he expect his laird – Aikhowe – to want it? And there's more.' He filled his mouth with the last food from his plate and, while he chewed, he flipped the pages of one of his books. 'Here we are,' he said, swallowing. 'In seventeen thirty-four, the year before Laird's Tam Elliot was hanged, a certain Tom Elwood – the name Elwood was a variant of Elliot – was taken after a pursuit of more than two weeks. His crime was waylaying a traveller.'

'Was the traveller killed?' Paul asked.

'Of course. Well, that crime became a local pastime. In the days of the reivers, the traveller was usually left alone. Later, the usual attitude was that it served him right for venturing into the Borders without adequate protection. A pursuit of over a fortnight suggests that the traveller must have been of more than ordinary importance. Elwood was taken to Carlisle but there's no further record of him – perhaps because of the alternative spelling of the names.'

'That checks with what I told you,' Paul pointed out.

'Yes. But there's another story which I've always believed may have been connected.' Keith picked up the other book but without opening it. 'At that time, Scottish weaponry was at its peak. Sword- and gun-making were virtually stamped out later, after the Forty-five Rebellion. When they recovered they had lost their individuality. But early in the eighteenth century, even the Czar of all the Russias – Peter the Great – ordered his sword-hilts from Glasgow or Stirling and pistols from Doune. He'd studied shipbuilding in England – remember?' – the others nodded their heads wisely – 'so he'd have met up with work from the different gun centres.'

Keith let the book in his hand fall open. 'This is a rather rare book about certain royal armouries. I picked it up at a sale, years ago. Peter the Great's guns and swords are inventoried, but there's an interesting footnote. "In 1735, Czar Peter sent his envoy to Berwick with orders to commission pistols from Alex Campbell of Doune and sword-hilts from Walter Allan of Stirling, but the envoy never returned." I've another book, which I can't put my hand on for the moment, in which the writer suggests that the envoy decamped with what would have been a considerable amount of money.'

'But you think,' Paul said slowly, 'that Laird's Tam might have knocked off the Russian envoy and taken the goodies.'

'It would make sense. Berwick must mean Berwick-on-Tweed, not North Berwick. If the envoy was heading back there to take ship, he'd pass this way. And if Laird's Tam had knocked off the Russian envoy, it would explain the hunt being kept up for a fortnight.'

'But surely,' Molly said, 'word would have got back to the Czar?'

'Not if the Constable at Carlisle, or some other official, had frozen onto what was left of the money.'

'Or the weapons,' Paul said. 'Or do you suspect that they're still around, buried some place.'

'Some of them,' Keith said. 'They've never shown up in any collection, public or private, that I've been able to trace. That would explain why he sent a Bible to Aikhowe. "There's monie a muckle truth hid in its pages." '

'They'd be valuable?' Paul asked.

Deborah, in suitably reverent tones said, 'The last good pair of Doune pistols to come on the open market fetched the equivalent of a quarter of a million dollars.'

'Now that,' Paul said, 'is valuable.'

'I wouldn't want to kid you,' Keith said. 'It's unlikely that the arms are intact and even unlikelier that we could find them. But I wouldn't swindle you either. You see, if that Bible still exists I just might make a guess at where it is. I could have gone after it on my own. But would you be interested in following it up with me, on a fifty-fifty basis?'

'You mean, splitting the value at sale?' Paul asked.

'Don't do it,' Molly advised him quickly. 'When Keith gets his hands on goods of that sort, somehow they never make it to the sale-room. He just can't bear to part with them. He'll deny it, but he's a collector before he's a businessman.'

'Long before,' Deborah said.

'I sympathise. All I want out of it is an antique pistol for the wall,' Paul said. 'A piece of history with my ancestor's name attached. So we share out the goodies. Who gets first pick?'

'I do,' Keith said. 'You'll never get there without my help.'

'And with it?'

'If they're still where Laird's Tam left them,' Keith said, 'I think that I could have a chance of finding those weapons with or without your help.'

Paul looked down at his fingers. When he looked up again, he said, 'A pair of pistols counts as two items?'

It was Keith's turn to hesitate. 'We shouldn't split a pair,' he said at last. 'But as long as we keep in touch so that they could be brought together again . . . '

For the first time, Paul Cardinal smiled. 'I said I was a gambler. You've got yourself a deal.'

The sound of a telephone bell stopped conversation in its tracks, drowning thoughts even of a treasure trove of royal arms. The nearest phone was in Keith's study, across the hall. Quickly as Keith moved, Deborah was in front of him, the wind of her passing scattering the petals from a vase of flowers. When he arrived in the doorway she was already speaking, her voice shrill with excitement.

'Yes, of course we'll accept the call,' she said, and then, 'Ian!' she cried. 'Oh, Ian! Where are you? Are you all right? What's been happening? Why hasn't anybody heard—?'

Keith felt his heart lift with relief, for Deborah more than for Ian Fellowes. Gently, he detached her from the phone. Deborah was laughing and crying. Her mother held her warmly.

'Let's have it,' Keith said briefly into the phone. He listened for a long minute. 'I'll tell the Chief Super and I'll get somebody to square things with the boat's owner,' he said. He looked up. 'Ian's with a boat,' he said. 'He's come by some very important evidence and a vital witness, both of them implicating a criminal big-shot. He thinks that every hard man in the country may be on the lookout for him. Perhaps he's being paranoid, but perhaps not.' He spoke into the phone again. 'You could be right. One venal coastguard could put you back into danger. Do as you said. Get out to the islands and I'll come for you – hire another boat from Berwick or something.'

He felt a tug at his sleeve and looked round. Paul Cardinal was leaning over him. 'I still have some contacts around here,' Paul said. 'And money's no great concern. If I whistle up a chopper, do I get first pick of the Czar's weapons?'

'We'll toss a coin.'

'You're on.'

'You were right,' Keith said. 'You are a gambler.' Into the phone he said, 'We're getting a helicopter. I don't know how long it'll take. When you see it, head in towards the beach at Bamburgh.'

Deborah tried to wriggle out of her mother's clutches. 'I want to speak to him.'

'We don't want the phone tied up,' Keith said. 'And Ian's got to get out of Lindisfarne before the causeway uncovers.' He disconnected.

'Well, I want to come with you.'

Paul Cardinal shook his head. 'We're not talking Sikorski,' he said. 'All I'll be able to get in a hurry's a small four-person job; and there's two to collect.'

'You're going to wash your face in cold water and lie down, my girl,' Molly said. This was her panacea for over-excitement in the family. She packed Deborah off upstairs. Paul was already on the telephone.

Molly jerked her head and retired to the kitchen. Keith joined her. 'I'm tempted to keep Munro in the dark until the midnight deadline,' he said. 'Teach him a lesson. But he might jump the gun. I'll call him as soon as the phone's free.'

Molly had more important matters on her mind. 'You'll have to go with Paul in the helicopter,' she said.

'Me?' Keith said. 'Not for the world!'

'Think about it.'

'If I think about it I'll . . . I'll . . . '

'Mess your pants,' Molly said briskly. 'Yes, I know you're terrified of flying, but this is important. What do you really know about Paul Cardinal?'

'Only that he really is Paul Cardinal, ex-LAPD.'

'And that he's American and he turned up here at the very moment Ian escaped with a witness and evidence against an American, and he arrived with just the sort of story most calculated to catch your attention. Is it so impossible that a retired Los Angeles policeman would turn professional hit-man?'

89

'But—'

'If he's what he says he is, why would he go to all the expense of hiring a helicopter to rescue somebody he's never met?' Molly persisted. 'To get first pick of a treasure that's probably rusted away by now, somewhere nobody'll ever find it? Be your age! If he can whistle up a helicopter at a moment's notice, we'll know that he made arrangements in advance.'

Keith wanted to protest, not because her reasoning was unsound but because his only concept of hell took the form of an endless flight in a small helicopter. But before he could find any fresh arguments, they heard Paul Cardinal calling from the study. They went through together.

'I got one,' Paul said. (Molly tried to catch Keith's eye but he refused to make eye contact.) 'An old friend in the oil industry can help out. When and where shall I tell him to come?'

Keith looked at the study clock. Daylight would be fading before they could hope to get to Holy Island and back. He had no intention of blundering around in the dark in the hands of a pilot of unknown capability. 'First light,' he said. 'Tell him two miles north of Newton Lauder. There's a flat field near here, between the main and the local roads. We'll spread a white sheet.'

Paul relayed the instructions.

Deborah had come downstairs again. 'I've washed,' she said defiantly, 'but I couldn't lie down. I want to go with the helicopter.'

'Well, you can't,' Keith said. He swallowed. 'I'm going with Paul and there won't be a spare seat.'

'*You're* going? But what about—?'

'What about nothing,' Keith said. If he was not firm, he was going to chicken out. 'I'm going and that's that. If you want something useful to keep you occupied while we're away, go and see Charlie and find out if that Bible's still in existence.'

'Charlie?' Paul said. 'Who's Charlie?'

'He's the Earl of Jedburgh. An old beau of Deborah's. His family name was Ilwand, which is another archaic spelling of Elliot. His seat is at Aikhowe.'

Keith escaped upstairs and burrowed into a cupboard in the gunroom. There was a Browning automatic in there somewhere, still in its original wrapping.

Paul regarded Deborah with increased respect. 'So you could've been a . . . a . . . '

'Countess,' Deborah said. 'Yes, I could. But I think I'd rather be a detective's wife.'

'You don't know what you're taking on,' Paul said.

Six

Lonely Lady, moored to the disused lifeboat slipway at Holy Island, nodded gently while they bickered over their next move. Ian's head moved restlessly, watching for the appearance of an enemy above the skyline of the Heugh, the escarpment which screens the natural harbour. For the moment, they could have been alone in the world.

Now that she had reached shore unscathed, Sheila was scenting the delights of hot baths, fresh food and a stable floor under her feet and she was reluctant to face the sea again. 'Surely,' she said, 'now that you've phoned your chief and put my sketch in the post, the danger's over. Isn't it? We've done what they were trying to stop us doing, if they ever did do more than chase us along the beach.'

Ian took her points one at a time. 'Not my chief,' he said. 'I have two of them. The one I'm doing this for would think twice and then call on the coastguard – and if Dora has friends in that quarter we could literally be sunk. I phoned somebody I can trust. As to danger being over, maybe and maybe not. We know what we've done, but if there's anybody after us they may not wait to find out before doing whatever they've been told to do. And your sketch would mean very little in evidence if you weren't there to speak to it.'

'But there wasn't anybody here,' Sheila said, not for the first time.

'There could be, five minutes after the causeway

uncovers. There would be, if I were in Dora's shoes. Maybe I'm wrong. Maybe we were never in any danger. But in view of the disaster for Dora if our evidence comes out, I'm not prepared to take chances on it. Now that we have food and water and clothes and fuel for the outboard—'

'Clothes of a sort. Your . . . your friend is going to the police, isn't he?'

'Of course. But he'll speak to the right person at the right time. I'm glad now that we didn't send any message by another boat – we could have raised a storm.

'I've got my instructions. He's going to smooth things over with the owner of *Lonely Lady*. I'm to get the hell out of harm's way until he can send a helicopter to pick me up. That could take time, if the choppers are all busy. After that, if you come along for another ride, we can tuck you away somewhere safe while the whole complex mess unravels.'

'Wouldn't I be safe if I phoned for a car to take me away?' Sheila asked wistfully. 'I couldn't pay for it,' she added.

Ian was tired of doing her thinking for her while he was anxiously trying to think for himself. 'Don't worry about the cost of a car,' he said. 'Have it on me, if you've made up your mind. Personally, I wouldn't take the risk, but you're a big girl. If that's what you want to do, go ahead.' He began to take the tiers off the mainsail. 'I'm sailing, before somebody can come over the causeway with a rifle. He may be watching the mainland end now, nursing a gun, or he may not. I can't tell you for sure,' he added more gently, 'and I can't make up your mind for you. But I'm leaving now.'

Sheila looked up at the Heugh. At that distance and without her glasses it was little more than a smudge. That decided her. If danger threatened, it would be all the more terrifying, coming unseen out of a blur. She found that she would rather face the sea again with a

93

sharp-eyed protector than the dangers of the land alone. 'I'm coming,' she said.

They motored out of the large, natural harbour through the narrowing channel, past the small castle on its conical hill, keeping the beacons lined up astern. The outgoing tide swept them along.

From his position on the mainland, Jimmy Jay only saw the tip of the masthead, but he ground his teeth at the sight. Of all the yachts on the coast, Sod's Law dictated that this would be the one. Too late now to redeem himself with Dora. He decided to crawl into a hole and not to come out until the shit had stopped flying, if ever.

Two hours of motor-sailing in light airs brought *Lonely Lady* to the Farne Islands. Ian fetched out a long warp and a CQR anchor and they brought up in the Kettle, an anchorage sheltered by the low humps of Knox Reef, West Wideopen and Farne Island itself. Ian pointed out the escape route to the south offered by Wideopen Gut.

Sheila, still hankering for the comforts of land, was in a peevish mood. 'I think,' she said primly, 'that that's the most disgusting place-name I ever heard.'

'Perhaps you're right,' Ian said. 'But it's very suitable.' As their ordeal neared an end and tiredness took over from tension, he began to feel lightheaded. 'If anyone comes at us from seaward, I'll be through there like a dose of salts.'

Sheila gasped, giggled and then threw back her head. They laughed together. Seals, looking like earless Labradors, came to the surface to see what the noise was about.

They luxuriated in a leisurely meal of the best that Holy Island had been able to offer, eaten from cracked plates with plastic cutlery that seemed to have originated with some airline. Then each took a turn on watch while the other struggled in the cramped space below to wash and change into the jeans and T-shirts which had been all that the local shop could find in their respective sizes. It would have been easier on deck but, although their privacy seemed complete, they could have been in the binoculars of lighthousemen or birdwatchers. Messages might now be flying to Dora, but Ian thought not and he was becoming too tired to care.

After a night and more than a day of constant and sometimes frantic activity, there was a sudden peace. Their world was a huge globe of still water and still, clear air. They sat in the cockpit, dozing or chatting desultorily. Sheila had acquired a writing-pad to replace her sketching block. When she had finished as detailed a portrait of the American as her memory, assisted by Ian's, could manage, she began to fill the pad with sketches of Bamburgh Castle, romantically dominating the skyline from two miles off, and then of the seals which came round the boat in friendly quest for fish offal. She found that a seal's face lent itself to a wide variety of expressions.

'So when do we expect this helicopter?' she asked suddenly.

Ian Fellowes jerked out of a half-sleep. 'They don't wait around like taxis,' he said. 'At least, I don't think they do.'

'I suppose not.' Sheila looked up from a vigorous sketch of her companion. She had drawn him twice as a seal but was now portraying him as himself. If he had seen it, which he never did, he might have been surprised to see who he could appear in the eyes of a lady of romantic temperament. Without distorting the truth by more than a hair's breadth, Sheila had straightened his nose and added to the firmness of his jaw. She had also given to his brow a serene nobility which was usually lacking. She had drawn a head that would have looked well above armour and a white horse but it was still recognisably Ian Fellowes. 'A ride in a helicopter will be another new experience,' she said. 'Is it coming here?'

'This is a bird sanctuary. If we landed a chopper here we'd have every wildlifer in the country up in arms. I said to overfly us and then to pick us up from the beach below Bamburgh Castle.'

'We can't just abandon somebody's boat.'

'He'll have her collected, probably by somebody from Seahouses—'

'From where?'

'From North Sunderland. Over there,' he said, pointing lazily. 'They call it Seahouses. Or the pilot may bring a man with him. She'll be returned to the owner with apologies and enough of a cheque to poultice any wounded feelings. I'm more concerned about just who'll pay the bill at the end of the day.'

Time wore on without any sign of the promised helicopter. Mist crept low over the water, drawing unreality over the scene. The sun dipped for the short midsummer night. Neither of them cared to doss down in the squalid conditions below. Instead, they brought up the bunk cushions and the only two blankets and huddled down on the cockpit sole, sheltering from a night which had become suddenly colder. A heavy slop came rolling in from the north-east, product of a depression over the distant fjords, and *Lonely Lady* turned broadside to it and tried to roll her mast out.

With no distraction for their minds, their bodies were vulnerable. Soon, Sheila threw off the blanket and hung miserably over the side. Ian got up and used the heavy water carrier as a weight, sending it up the mast on the main halliard so that the boat's period of roll would no longer synchronise with the seaway. The rolling reduced, but too late. In his turn, Ian knelt and surrendered.

When the worst of the miseries were past, they huddled down again in their nest, shivering and clinging together for warmth and comfort. The mood of mutual dependence, at a time when every circumstance was unfamiliar, bore them along. Small liberties led to greater and, when

96

these were accepted and returned, they found themselves, without conscious intent, joined in the ultimate embrace.

Fear and nausea were forgotten. Sheila was due, or long overdue, for some bodily loving. Her one previous affair, entered into out of a sense of duty to her chosen lifestyle, had been brief, physically painful and totally unsatisfying. Ian's lingering inhibitions and the discomfort of the cockpit sole combined to postpone his achievement of release. It was a revelation to Sheila that a man – even one who, she still half believed, was a member of a profession noted for its talent in such matters – could restrain himself for so long for her greater pleasure. She came at last to an orgasm which she could only describe to herself as mind-blowing. Later, she tried to paint it, but doing it, in her own opinion, far less than justice. The painting, mostly depicting coloured bubbles, resembled an explosion in a factory making washing-up liquid.

They fell asleep at last, heedless of any possible dangers, and woke to a bright dawn and the clatter of the helicopter passing high overhead on course for Bamburgh Castle. The noise put thousands of seabirds into the air and guano pattered around them like rain.

They adjusted their clothing without looking at each other, and made sail.

Harry Skoll was ostensibly an inshore fisherman working out of North Sunderland, but the largest part of his living came from the theft of expensive gear off the yachts at Blyth and around the Tyne. This he passed to Mary Bruce, for disposal through contacts on the Clyde, receiving in return payments impenetrably disguised as racing windfalls or the proceeds from the sale of shellfish.

He believed, quite wrongly, that the ladies had always treated him fairly. So when he recognised Foxy's voice on the phone, he was willing to branch out. For a hundred a day per person, he would keep a watch out for *Lonely Lady*; and, if he should make contact with her, he would destroy boat and crew, for an agreed fee plus legal expenses if required. He would, he said, take three men and work a shift system.

He waited for dark in order to obscure the identifying numbers on his lobster boat, and went out in her alone. An extra three hundred pounds per day was hardly to be passed up, and Harry Skoll's experience of yachtsmen did not suggest that they would be formidable opponents. When *Lonely Lady* at last poked her bow out from behind Farne Island, he had been at the helm for more than twenty-four hours and he was close to exhaustion. In such ways can incompetence and greed undermine the most thorough planning.

An hour earlier, the lights of a yacht approaching from the direction of the Tweed had boosted him into wakefulness with a surge of adrenalin. The newcomer had turned out to be a white ketch, twice the size of his quarry. This alarm past, he had sunk back into torpor and, although the appearance of *Lonely Lady*'s sails, ghosting slowly in the light breeze, coincided with the Farne Islands' end of his patrol, he nearly ignored her and was in the act of turning away before his sluggish mind took note of the evidence of his eyes. He swung onto a converging course and fumbled in the case of bottles at his feet. He had decided that petrol bombs, on the lines of Molotov cocktails, offered the best and most suitable weaponry, and the cheapest.

Sergeant Fellowes had been on the go for longer than had Harry Skoll and although he had had some sleep he had also had Sheila Blayne. He was swimming through a sludge of exhaustion to which he was giving way as he neared his journey's end. He hardly noticed the other boat until, with nightmare shock, he realised that she was coming down purposefully on his port quarter. He reached behind him to start the outboard motor and, as the little engine spluttered into life and kicked *Lonely Lady* forward, he gybed. *Lonely Lady* spun on her heel.

When Skoll looked up, ready to throw, he found his quarry away on his beam. He put his helm over and swung in again, closer this time. His first petrol bomb went through the gap between main- and foresail, trailing a whisper of flame, as Ian gybed again. The lobster boat passed *Lonely Lady*'s stern and Skoll had time to throw a second bottle which left an arc of burning petrol on the mainsail before narrowly missing the deck and plopping into the sea. Sheila, who had been rapidly learning the way of boats, eased the foresail sheets and they bustled away towards the shore again.

Sheila had had more sleep than Ian and, being less concerned about such matters as wind changes and dragging anchors, had slept more deeply. Her experiences of the night had also induced in her a state of relaxation. As a result, while Ian responded mechanically to the need for evasive action, Sheila, whose usual reaction would have been to wring her hands and whimper, was both alert and calm enough to think constructively about deterrence and retaliation. She pulled the two-gallon can, still half full of petrol, from under the cockpit seat and loosened the cap.

Harry Skoll came in again, on the lee side this time to prevent another gybe. Ian saw him approaching but his mind refused to come up with any more answers. He looked back and, unaccountably, yawned.

That yawn was Harry Skoll's undoing. His first assault on an unsuspecting quarry might have succeeded. But in the letdown after the earlier alarm his body, like Ian's, was out of adrenalin. Tiredness was resuming control. In the face of Ian's cavernous yawn, his own face convulsed in sympathy. His jaw clicked, his ears popped and, more crucially, his watering eyes clamped shut. His response was so total that his aim faltered. The throw would have passed harmlessly above the cockpit and below the boom except that Ian, opening his eyes to the near passage of a missile, instinctively put up a hand and caught it, stared for a moment in horror at the inverted bottle and threw it back again. With the strength of desperation, Sheila followed up with the petrol can.

The two boats were close and parallel and even the wildest throw could hardly have missed by more than a few inches. Harry Skoll, caught between the after-effects of his yawn and the need to duck beneath a bottle which nearly split his head open, failed at first to take in the significance of the can which had landed at his feet, spraying a gout of petrol over his surroundings and himself, and was now gurgling into the bilges. He was on the point of striking his lighter to ignite the rope fuse in another missile when he realised that he was now steering a potential fireball. He got rid of the nearly empty can over the side and circled away. He was furious, outraged. This was dastardly, dangerous, outwith the rules.

Petrol-bombing might be out but ramming was definitely in. The lobster boat was the larger of the two and of much the heavier construction. They were nearing the shore but there was still time and water enough to sink them and then to kill the two somehow, anyhow. If all else failed, he was ready to rip them to pieces with his teeth and toenails.

Even in his wrath at the infringement of his copyright, Skoll had more sense than to approach again on *Lonely Lady*'s lee. Although the petrol on the sail had burnt away and the damp and salty canvas was unwilling to do more than smoulder, sparks were still raining onto the water. But the petrol fire had taken a large bite out of the mainsail which now hung and flapped loosely, spilling the breeze. *Lonely Lady* was slowing and sluggish. Skoll had time to circle to windward. Then he opened the throttle of his diesel and let his speed build up.

Ian had little sail to aid his manoeuvrability and he was losing speed. In desperation, he let the foresail sheet fly and put the outboard astern. *Lonely Lady* stopped dead and even made a little sternway against the draw of the remaining canvas. Skoll glanced off her bow and circled

100

to come in again, yelling unintelligible curses in broadest Northumbrian.

Ian gave himself up for lost and braced himself for the impact. Sheila waited confidently for whatever rabbit he might next pull out of the hat.

With a whoosh and a clatter the helicopter came overhead, flattening a disc of sea with its wind. Ian saw a stranger in the open doorway. Keith's face, very white and with staring eyes, was visible through the perspex. A rock the size of a football hit the sea and a column of water shot up between the two boats.

Harry Skoll leaned on his helm and bore away. Even Dora could not expect him to continue his attack in the teeth of dive-bombing. He headed east, yawning enormously and shaking his fist. He knew of a secluded anchorage beyond Staples Island where he could pump out the petrol and restore his boat's identity before heading for the Tyne to establish an alibi.

Lonely Lady's keel grounded gently on the sand. Ian kicked the anchor over the side and they half swam and half waded ashore. The helicopter was down a hundred yards away, its blades still idling round, and two men were stepping down.

Ian turned to Sheila and put out his hand. 'By God,' he said, 'we made it!'

Sheila took the hand, looked down and gave a squeak of horror. Ian saw for the first time that the sleeve of his oilskin jacket was burned away and that the skin of his wrist and forearm was blistered and charred.

It began to hurt. It hurt like hell.

Back at the helicopter, Keith produced his Browning from the belt holster, led Paul Cardinal out from under the circling blades and patted him over. If the American had a weapon on him it was only a tiny penknife.

'No hard feelings?' Keith said.

The American shrugged. 'It wasn't the first time I've been searched,' he said. 'Felt quite like old times.'

There was little said on the flight to Newton Lauder. Even if the noise of the engine and rotor had permitted conversation, Ian and Sheila were dozing, Keith was holding the machine in the air by sheer willpower, the pilot was busy and Paul Cardinal had lapsed into silence. But from the moment the helicopter touched down in the field near Briesland House, everybody seemed to be talking at once.

Chief Superintendent Munro, who had been warned by a radio message, was waiting with a uniformed sergeant beside an ambulance, his face split by an unaccustomed grin of delight. Molly was almost dancing around him in impatience to see that Keith had survived undamaged, but Ian Fellowes was first to descend carefully to the ground.

'Into the ambulance,' Munro said. 'I'll come up and talk to you at the hospital. Go with him, Sergeant Duffus.' His words were abrupt and his face was sober again but Keith, knowing the Chief Superintendent well, could see the spring in his step and hear the lilt in his voice. Mr Munro was in the grip of overwhelming relief.

'Yes, of course,' Ian said. He allowed himself to be led in the direction of the ambulance but he was looking at Molly. 'Where's Deborah?' he asked her.

Keith had followed him to the ground. He was marking time to reassure himself that he really was back on terra firma. 'I gave her an errand to do, to keep her busy. And I told her that we wouldn't be back here before midday, so that she'd stay out from under our feet. You don't want to be fussed over. You'll see her soon enough.'

Sergeant Fellowes would have liked nothing better than to be fussed over by Deborah, but duty called. 'Sir,' he said. Munro, who had been snapping orders at Sergeant Duffus, looked at him. 'Miss . . . I've forgotten her surname.'

102

'Blayne,' Sheila said plaintively from the doorway of the helicopter.

'Miss Blayne has a sketch of the American, presumably the client for the special weapon. And – Mrs Calder – you'll look after her until some arrangement can be made?'

'She will be looked after,' Munro said firmly. 'Now go.'

'Yes, of course.' But Ian stood where he was. 'Is Superintendent McHarg on the way?'

'Not yet.'

'He's been informed?'

'He will be,' Munro said blandly. 'I have left a message asking him to call me back. No doubt he will do so, one of these days. If he cares to be discourteous, he can hardly blame me if he is the last person to hear the good news.'

Ian took two more paces towards the ambulance and stopped again. 'Keith, the boat . . . '

'Leave it to me.'

Paul Cardinal had been engaged in discussion with the pilot. Some paper changed hands. As the ambulance pulled away, the helicopter drowned all other sound and rose into the air. Molly clutched her hair. Sheila waved with the hand that held her note-pad. The sound began to die.

'Now, Miss Blayne,' Munro said. 'You will come with me and make a statement.'

'Couldn't I have a bath and some clean clothes first?' Sheila asked. 'Please? Mrs Calder?'

Molly, who had at last accepted Keith's assurance that both he and Ian Fellowes were sound in wind and limb – apart from some slight scorching of the Sergeant – recognised a *cri de coeur*. She quite understood that no woman could bear to venture into a man's world unwashed and in quite the wrong clothes. 'Of course,' she said. 'Come into the house. It needn't take long,' she told Munro.

The Chief Superintendent faltered. He knew Molly

103

of old, and the fact that he was desperate to obtain the evidence, notify all other forces and then crow over McHarg would mean nothing to her compared to offering the necessary female comforts to another woman. 'Well, be quick,' he said weakly. 'And give me that sketch before you go.'

Sheila handed over her note-pad. Munro looked down at the square face, drawn with so lucid a hand as to be more than photographically believable. It was alive.

Paul Cardinal was looking over Munro's shoulder. 'Hey! I know that guy,' he said.

Munro looked up at him. 'Oh, it's you,' he said repressively. 'The policeman from Los Angeles.'

'From the Anti-terrorist Task Force,' Keith said.

'I put him away,' Paul said. 'It should have been for life but it got plea-bargained down to near zilch. You've got a tough one there.'

Munro brightened. A positive identification of the assassin would be another feather in his cap. 'Tell me,' he said.

'You can all stand here if you want to,' said Keith. 'I'm going into the house. I've got to do something about that bloody boat.'

Sheila Blayne, clean, rosy and very much refreshed, came out of the bathroom in a borrowed dressing-gown. Molly called her into Deborah's bedroom where, laid out on the bed, was a selection of clothes, chosen not so much as being suitable for Sheila but as being unsuitable for Deborah, comprising dresses too young or too old or too revealing for one of Deborah's years or unsuited to her colouring; and underwear which Molly condemned, in her own mind, as 'tarty'.

When she heard the buzz of the hair dryer cease, Molly returned. 'Do you mind if we talk while you get dressed?' she asked. 'Mr Munro's itching to whisk you away and we may not get another chance.'

Sheila dragged Deborah's brush through her hair and regarded herself unhappily in the dressing-table mirror. 'Of course I don't mind,' she said.

Molly took a seat on the bed. 'It's a romantic story,' she said. 'If I've got it right, you were in the hands of these crooks and they were going to kill you, when Ian Fellowes came along like a knight on a white charger and rescued you. Is that what happened?'

'Something like that,' Sheila mumbled. She avoided meeting Molly's eye in the mirror.

'When I was' – Molly nearly said *your age* but changed it quickly – 'very young, I dreamed of something like that happening to me. I was going to fall in love with my rescuer and live happily for ever after.'

'And did it happen?' Sheila asked her.

This question, arising from what had been no more than an oblique approach to a difficult subject, nearly threw Molly; but she recovered quickly. 'I don't know,' she said, 'I haven't lived for ever yet. You could say that Keith came to my rescue once or twice, but I loved him before that. It would be natural for you to get romantic ideas about Ian. And for him to get ideas about you. The knight always fell in love with the maiden in distress. But it probably turned out to be a terrible mistake.'

Sheila's hair looked like a dishmop but she put down the brush. 'You don't have to worry about that,' she said. 'Honestly you don't. In real life, the knight was probably in love with his horse. I know that he's sort of engaged to your daughter. He told me that.' She decided not to mention that Ian had only made his revelation after their interlude on the cockpit sole.

'I'm glad. They're very well suited and very much in love. I couldn't bear it if Deborah lost Ian just as life's opening up for her.'

'That won't happen,' Sheila said. 'I saw his face when she didn't meet the helicopter.' She came over to the bed, clutching the dressing-gown together. 'These are expensive clothes. Are you sure it's all right . . . ?'

'Keep anything that takes your fancy,' Molly said. 'Deb always was extravagant about clothes but she never knows what will suit her. I . . . I saw your face while you were watching his. I accept what you say, of course, but something happened between you, didn't it?'

Sheila clutched the dressing-gown tighter for a moment and then, as though deciding that the quicker she got dressed the sooner she could escape from this inquisition, she took it off and draped it carefully across the bed. 'Nothing that matters,' she said.

'My dear,' Molly said as if speaking to a child, 'I haven't brought up a daughter without learning to recognise whether something matters or not. I wouldn't want to see any one of the three of you hurt.'

'Honestly . . . ' Sheila choked.

'Honestly?'

Sheila sat down again and hung her head. 'It was my fault,' she whispered. 'It shouldn't have happened. But we were cold after being seasick and it was all strange and quiet and sort of ghostly, rather like that poem about "Drifting across a sea of dreams to a haunted shore of song". And I was still afraid. I only wanted somebody warm and strong to hold onto. I didn't mean anything to happen and nor did he. But it seemed natural and inevitable at the time. And in a way beautiful. But now I think he's ashamed. That's the only bit of it that hurts.' Her whisper faded away.

Molly was not shocked. She could not have been first Keith's mistress and then his wife without learning more than a little about human frailty and the pains which it can bring in its wake. Keith in his day had been a notorious philanderer. She was fairly sure that Ian and Deborah had not yet established a physical relationship. From her knowledge of men in general and Keith in particular, she would not have expected Ian Fellowes to live the life of a monk. The question in her mind

106

was whether Sheila was right and the incident 'did not matter'.

'What about you?' she asked. 'Are you ashamed?'

'No, I'm not,' Sheila said after a moment of thought. There was both surprise and defiance in her voice.

'That's good. But what comes next?'

Sheila shrugged. 'Nothing comes next. What happened is over. If things had been different . . . but they aren't. I . . . I'm an artist. Well, an art student. I think I may be a real artist some day. In my year, most of the girls have affairs. They seem to break up and get over it. I'll do the same.'

'Your heart isn't broken, then? I think you're being very sensible. I shan't say anything to anybody and I suggest very strongly that you do the same – with one exception. You're the only person who could suggest to Ian that he must say nothing to Deborah.'

'He wouldn't, would he?'

'He could, as a sort of confessional. Hoping to be forgiven, which he might not be. So you must be firm.'

Sheila sighed. 'You're right. Thank you,' she said. 'Thank you very much, Mrs Calder. I think that you're the sensible one. It's not every mother who could discuss things so calmly and reasonably and come to the right answer. My mother certainly couldn't.'

'I hope it really is the right answer. And now,' Molly said, 'you'd better hurry up. Wash your face with cold water and finish dressing. Mr Munro will be pacing up and down the hall by now. But come back when he's finished with you. We can give you a bed, just until we can be sure that it's safe for you to go home.'

'But would I have to meet Sergeant Fellowes again? And your daughter? I'm not sure that I could face them.'

'You can do it,' Molly said. 'You must. You'll be amazed what you can do if you really try. If you rush off now, where would you go? Back to Dundee? Ian might be worried enough to chase after you and then the cat would be in the fire.' Molly was going to say more but she had lost herself in her medley of metaphors. Enough was enough. She smiled vaguely and left the room.

Outside the bedroom door, she leaned her head against the wall and took several deep breaths.

Chief Superintendent Munro had finished for the moment with Paul Cardinal and was, as Molly had suggested, lurking in the hall. He was muttering rude comments in Gaelic about the time some women spent in prettying themselves. As soon as Sheila descended the stairs, he swept her off to Newton Lauder.

Keith, meanwhile, had managed to contact by telephone a sailing friend who could collect *Lonely Lady*, returning her to the Tay and coming back with the van. He hung up, after a lengthy wrangle over the costs of fuel and subsistence, and looked up to find that Paul Cardinal was standing in the study doorway.

'Come and join me, if you aren't in a huff,' Keith said. He yawned. In his youth, a very few hours of dozing in an armchair would have sufficed him for a night's sleep but he was getting older and, he told himself severely, softer. 'You'll take a drink?'

'I certainly will.' Paul lowered himself into one of the deep armchairs. 'I never got used to your British beers. I could use a Scotch, if you keep it.'

'I'll join you. It's early, but this isn't an ordinary day. I don't feel like settling down to work. I might take a gun out later and try for a few rabbits.' An old shooting friend with Customs and Excise kept Keith supplied with a single malt which had never been subject to duty. He poured two large drams, added a touch of water and resumed his seat. 'Try that for size.'

Paul sipped and then drank. 'It fits,' he said. 'That's really something. No, I'm not in a pet. I was expecting it. I knew you didn't trust me all the way.'

Keith nearly spilled his drink. 'What made you think that?'

'You learn to notice things, like the way somebody never lets you get behind him, the shape under a coat and the way the weight of a pistol in a holster makes a man carry his shoulder different. Most of all, just the look in a man's eyes.' Paul's face was still expressionless. 'You've taken it off now.'

'With both the witnesses now surrounded by police, it seemed to have become superfluous.'

'When we were dropping rocks from the chopper, you had your hand on it. Earlier, when we'd seen that they were being hassled and we set down on the shore to look for rocks, and again when we put down just now, you stayed behind me until you'd given me a frisking. I had the feeling that you were ready to gun me down if I tried anything. Am I right?'

'You're not far off.'

'I thought as much,' Paul said. 'I don't mind. I just took care to do nothing sudden. I'd've thought less of you if you hadn't been suspicious of a solitary American turning up here while there was an American hit-man on the loose. I don't match Miss Blayne's sketch, but you hadn't seen that at the time and anyways I could have been in cahoots with the assassin. But you reckon that I'd have made my move by now. Right?'

'That's right,' Keith said. To have his mind read aloud with such precision made him uncomfortable. 'Another dram?'

'Sure. Don't drop your guard too soon. They may have knocked off that gunsmith of yours, but we don't know how much he told them before he died. Have there been any strangers around?'

Keith put down the refilled glasses and shrugged. 'There are always visitors in summer, for the fishing. There's been one phone-call for me from somebody who didn't leave a message. Nothing out of the usual.'

109

Paul produced a faint trace of a smile. 'So maybe we can put it out of our minds now and get back to what I came to see you about. Tell me some more about that old ancestor of mine.'

'Give me time and don't hope for too much,' Keith said. 'Records were badly kept in those days and sometimes they were deliberately falsified. But I can think of one or two people I could ask.'

'I'd be grateful. If there's any question of a fee . . . '

'A bottle would be more than enough,' Keith said.

They were interrupted by the sound of Keith's jeep in the drive. It skidded to a halt on the gravel. The front door slammed and Deborah charged into the room. She had a parcel under her arm.

'Well?' she said. 'Well?'

'Your boyfriend's back,' Keith said. 'Safe and sound except for a little scorching here and there.'

Deborah looked hard at her father. 'This isn't your way of breaking it to me that he's already been cremated?'

Paul Cardinal choked on his whisky.

'Nothing like that,' Keith said.

A grin of relief spread over Deborah's face. 'Where is he?'

'Munro took him up to the hospital.'

The grin vanished. Deborah paled. 'I should be there,' she said.

'Relax,' Keith told her. 'He's probably back at work by now, showing off a bandage or two to the girls in between dictating an interminable statement full of the kind of jargon he thinks will impress his superiors. How did you get on?'

She dropped the parcel on her father's desk. 'This was in Charlie's library among the junk. More tatty old Bibles than you could shake a stick at. We think it's probably the right one, but if there are any secret messages in it we couldn't find them.' She turned back for the door.

'Don't you want to hear all about our morning?' Keith asked.

'Tell me later. I must see if I can catch up with Ian.' She vanished and they heard the jeep start up again.

'Young love,' Paul said tolerantly. 'Not a comfortable state, but I wish I could live it again. You know, if I'd wanted I could've taken that pistol off you.'

'That you couldn't,' Keith said.

'I could too. I used to teach that sort of combat.'

Keith put down his glass, empty again. 'Shall we look inside that parcel? Or shall we take that pistol outside, put a blank up the spout and see if you're suffering from delusions of adequacy?'

'Now that's a challenge I can't resist,' Paul said. 'What say a bottle of this whisky against ten of your pounds?'

Seven

Chief Superintendent Munro was enjoying himself far too much for Detective Superintendent McHarg's comfort.

Munro had played his cards with care and ingenuity, making full use of the good offices of the Assistant Chief Constable (Crime). The latter detested McHarg and had been pleased to set the seal on Munro's triumph by convening a hasty meeting in Edinburgh, attending it in person and then driving a coach and horses through all established protocol by insisting that Munro take the chair. Nearly twenty officers, of varying seniorities and specialities, had arrived from seven different forces, plus an observer from the Anti-terrorist Squad at Scotland Yard who had travelled up overnight and was in evident danger of falling asleep. Ian Fellowes was the most junior officer present.

Copies of the various statements had been distributed, but Munro led the Sergeant through his account, point by point. When they produced Sheila's drawing of the Tay with the figures in the foreground, an inspector from Strathclyde leaned forward.

'This is Dora Braddle to the life,' he said. 'With this and the two witnesses, even if the adapted rifle never surfaces, we can put her away for attempted kidnapping. When we find her,' he added soberly.

They heard the Sergeant out in silence to the end.

'But most of this . . . this farrago could be sheer paranoia,' McHarg said desperately. '"The wicked flee

when no man pursueth." The Sergeant here was stealing boats and running away from imagined dangers, but
the existence of a professional killer with a sophisticated
assassination weapon is the merest conjecture. And
there's no evidence of a massive coast-watch except for
one incident at sea which could have been a bit of bad
seamanship blown up out of all proportion.'

Ian Fellowes looked down at his white bandage but
held his peace.

'We experienced a statistical drop in the crime rate,'
said the man from Strathclyde. 'It seems that every known
hard man was out of the Region.'

'And we know where they were,' said a chief inspector
from Kirkcaldy. 'The harbourmasters are telling a con-
sistent story. There was somebody hanging around every
harbour-mouth. And they weren't waiting to buy fish.'

Somebody laughed.

'We'll move on,' Munro said. 'Sergeant Fellowes will
be available to answer questions later. Mr Cardinal is
waiting outside.' He nodded to Ian Fellowes, who went
to the door.

The inadequate room seemed even more crowded when
Paul Cardinal's bulk entered. The man from Strathclyde
had gained elbow-room by lighting a large pipe, but at
Munro's invitation the American pulled a spare chair into
the space.

'Mr Cardinal is a retired officer from the Los Angeles
Police Department and a former member of the Anti-
terrorist Task Force,' Munro said. The man from Scotland
Yard woke up suddenly.

Ian laid a copy of Sheila's sketch-portrait in front
of Paul. 'You know this man?' Munro asked him.

'I know him. Real name believed to be Raymond
Munster. Out of Philadelphia, of German extraction. I
won't trouble you with all the aliases he's used, because
he never uses the same one twice. Most probably he
uses the name of whoever's identification he's bought

113

or stolen. He started as a bodyguard to hoodlums who'd made the grade and he worked on up from there.'

'An example to any ambitious yuppy,' said the man from Strathclyde.

'You could say so. He's now a professional killer. More than twenty hits to his credit that we know of, but could be many more. He's worked for organised crime, for individuals, for activist organisations and for foreign powers – in fact, for whoever can afford his fees.'

'Go on,' Munro said.

'If you played your cards right, you could get his file over within a day.'

'A good photograph would help,' McHarg said.

Paul Cardinal laid a finger on a copy of Sheila Blayne's sketch-portrait. 'A photograph would only give you his physical appearance at one moment in the past. But this is the essence of the man. Off the top of the head, he's five-nine, a hundred and sixty pounds, nearing forty years old. Brown eyes. Hair brown, greying and receding, but that's easily changed. You want to know his *modus operandi*?'

'Too true,' said a voice.

'He works anywhere in the world but prefers English-speaking countries. He never carries weapons across borders so I guess you can count on his target being in Britain. He'll be lying low until his target's ready for him.'

Munro's friend, a superintendent in Tayside, said, 'With that picture circulated, we should be able to find him.'

'Maybe,' said Paul. 'But he has a knack of melting into his background. He's not great at languages but he's a wow at accents. Two days in a new place and he could pass for a native. His natural voice is deep but he's got a good range. A few minor changes to his appearance and a different voice and posture and you could walk right by him. No known weaknesses for drink or drugs or sex. Fussy about good food and he's a first-class cook when he has to look after himself.'

'What about this weapon?' asked the man from Strathclyde.

'Is it typical of his methods?'

'He's flexible,' Paul said. 'He's a good shot, doesn't need to depend on automatic weapons. You notice the case that's being handed over in the larger drawing? All credit to the young lady, she's got a sharp eye for details. Looks to me like a commercial camcorder case.'

'A recording video camera such as the TV people use?' the man from Scotland Yard said. 'I think you're right. Doesn't that suggest that his target's the sort of VIP who attracts the media?'

'It might,' Paul said thoughtfully. 'I guess you'll need to spread his picture around anywhere that'll get that sort of coverage. But notice that what she's drawn isn't the camcorder but the carrying case for one of them. If he'd intended to use it at a press conference, which is the only way he'd get close enough to a political big wheel or a head of state, he'd have had a target pistol built into the shell of a camcorder with the viewfinder acting as a telescopic sight. I've known that done.'

'He may have done that,' said the Assistant Chief Constable (Crime). 'The case could be holding it.'

Paul shook his head. 'A cut-down Ruger ten-twenty-two with a banana clip wouldn't fit,' he said. 'Most likely, he's using the camcorder case to get him into some area where the press and TV might be expected, like asking a big businessman for an interview. Or maybe he just figures that attaché cases are old hat. I wouldn't know. One thing I'm sure of, he'll want to test the weapon if he hasn't already.'

Munro made a note. 'A good point,' he said. 'But when this man is using a special weapon such as this adapted and concealed rifle, does he usually carry other weapons?'

115

'Not that I heard. He'd prefer to be able to dump the camcorder case and be clean. I can't promise, but I think that if you separate him from the case you can assume he's disarmed.'

Munro looked around the faces at the big table. 'I have asked Mr Cardinal to be available for the next day or two, in case we have more questions. But for now, I think that we should be discussing the measures to be taken. So unless there are any urgent questions for Mr Cardinal . . . '

'I'll say one thing more and then leave you in peace,' Paul said. 'Ray Munster's good at unarmed combat, but he isn't as good as he thinks he is. I nailed him good when he tried to knock off a visiting Colombian dignitary. He was convicted but he got off real light . . . and he's out again earlier than you'd expect. I told you that he's worked for all and sundry. I've heard it whispered that he's even done work for the CIA. Good morning, gentlemen.'

He left behind him the silence which falls when each man is afraid to say aloud the thought which is in each of their minds.

The ACC (Crime) decided that somebody had to voice it. 'If that wasn't a hint,' he said, 'I've never heard one. So among possible targets we must include anyone who might be unpopular with the US Government – along with those who may be disliked by Arabs or Israelis, the Irish, Libyans, Bulgarians, South Africans, big business, organised crime or any well-heeled bigot. I suggest that that can only be checked by local forces, because no central body keeps track of every person flying in to open a factory or have dinner with one of the Royals. We'll have to circulate every force in mainland Britain – every possible target and scrap of information to be reported back here. I suggest that Superintendent McHarg co-ordinates.'

McHarg scowled. 'If I could have the uninterrupted services of Sergeant Fellowes—'

116

'With respect . . . ' Ian Fellowes began. There was another quick silence. The words usually preceded some piece of gross impertinence.

The Sergeant was not anxious to meet Ray Munster again, but he was damned if he was going to hang around where Superintendent McHarg could vent his fury on him. 'I'm the only officer who's set eyes on this man Munster,' he said. 'I think that I should be available to join in observation if and when we pick up his trail again.'

'An excellent idea,' Munro said before McHarg could object. The ACC (Crime) nodded.

The Detective Superintendent tried to smile compliantly but he only succeeded in looking bilious.

Paul Cardinal, in his rented Jaguar, was back in Newton Lauder by the middle of the afternoon. He found Keith again behind the counter in the empty shop.

'Come in and keep me company,' Keith said. 'Otherwise I'll fall asleep and the shop will get robbed.'

The two men were becoming firm friends. The previous morning, after consuming most of the whisky bottle, they had adjourned to the garden for a contest to be settled by the best of three attempts by Paul to disarm Keith, but after two bouts, during which Keith had suffered bruised ribs and Paul's fingers had been scorched by the flame from the discharged blank, Molly had come out to read the Riot Act and the contest had been declared a draw. Of such episodes are friendships made.

Paul sat down in the customer's chair. 'I thought your partner was back from his vacation,' he said. 'I looked in here before I went to Edinburgh and there was a thin, intense-looking character looking after the place. He was determined to sell me a fishing rod.'

'That was Wal. But he's buggered off again for the moment, delivering clay pigeons to the Pentland Club, and our wives have gone to Kelso, shopping, taking Miss Blayne with them. So I'm lumbered. When do

117

you suppose it would be safe to let that young woman go home?'

'When Ray Munster and Dora Braddle are both in the slammer.'

'I suppose you're right,' Keith said glumly. Something about Sheila Blayne seemed to be troubling Molly and when Molly was troubled Keith knew that he would usually be troubled in his turn. 'How did the Edinburgh meeting go?'

'About what you'd expect. They bled me dry and tossed me out. Now they'll be wiring Miss Blayne's portrait of Ray Munster all over the country and advising other units to guard any prominent cookies as if they were the Ayatollah paying a call in Baghdad. Saturate any high ground, check media passes, cut down on contact with the public and all that jazz. And I guess they'll be trying to identify the target.'

'That'll be a long list.'

Paul nodded soberly. 'You always find that. But the list can be whittled down. If big bucks are going to change hands, bigger bucks are at stake. Except occasionally you find a millionaire with hatred in his gut. Well, it's not my kind of problem any longer. How's things in this neck of the woods?'

'Quiet,' Keith said. 'It always is at this time of year. If it wasn't for the fishermen and clay-busters, we'd starve. But I sold a good Browning this morning, which should keep the wolf from the door for today at least.'

'I'm glad to hear it. But I was more concerned to ask about that Bible your daughter brought back from Aikhowe.'

'I'd almost forgotten it, what with all the fuss and flapdoodle. Don't get your hopes too high. As I thought, the Earl of Jedburgh's a direct descendant of Ilwand of Aikhowe. The book date's about right. There's no saying that it's the right one, but Deborah's adamant that there was no other Bible there of that age. On the other hand, she's been through and through it. If there was ever a message tucked into the spine it's long gone and so has the spine.'

'What about marks in the text?' Paul asked. 'Words underlined?'

'Marks galore. What would you expect in a book more than two hundred years old? Whether any of them are significant Deborah hopes to discover. Between helping out at the Pentland Gun Club and following Ian Fellowes around like a mother hen, she's poring over the book as if it was the Holy Writ – which, of course, it is,' Keith added hastily. 'You realise that, if there ever was a message in it, Aikhowe may have discovered it and lifted any valuables while your ancestor was still up and kicking?'

Paul nodded. 'I know that. But you say there's been no sign of any of the pieces surfacing in museums?'

'True. But there are private collections. I've never seen the Queen's collection, for one. If the Constable of Carlisle grabbed anything, it might well have ended up in the royal collection.'

'It's still worth a try,' Paul said doggedly. 'Just imagine,' he said with more enthusiasm, 'one of those pistols hanging in a case over my mantelpiece and being able to say "My great-to-the-nth-power granddad was hanged for stealing that off the envoy of Czar Peter the Great." '

'A conversation stopper,' Keith admitted. 'But don't work up a head of steam just yet. Deborah spotted some tiny pinholes in the pages and she's tabulating them to see whether any message comes out. But, to start with, some of the pinholes may have closed up with the years while others may have been accidental. Then, there's nothing to say which side of the page they mark. And, again, a lot of the pages are missing. Finally, she's trying to recognise a message written by an eighteenth-century Scot in the dialect and with the highly eccentric spelling of the day, and referring to place-names which may have changed over the years.'

They were interrupted by a customer in search of a new reel for a trout rod. When they were alone again, Paul said, 'You got me worried now. You think they might have had some code arranged in advance, like "Only count every third pinhole and move up one letter every time"?'

'They might,' Keith said. 'But I can't see why they should. They couldn't have foreseen a need to pass secret messages.' He glanced up at the clock. 'Lowsing time, as we say. Could you fancy a Scotch over at the hotel?'

'That I could,' Paul said. 'I tried their Scotch last night and it couldn't hold a candle to that malt you gave me yesterday, but I guess I can make do.'

'You didn't know what to ask for,' Keith said. 'Wait while I lock up and then get your notebook out. You're due for another lesson in the superiority of malt Scotch over Bourbon.'

Ian Fellowes found himself firmly implanted in Chief Superintendent Munro's good books and enjoying the patronage of the ACC (Crime). For the moment, he was secure against the malice of Detective Superintendent McHarg. No doubt Mr McHarg would seek his revenge later, but the ACC (Crime) had hinted that changes were in the wind. Meantime, Ian had been admitted to the councils of his superiors.

An intelligence room had been set up in Edinburgh. They refused to call it an incident room on the theory that fate might be tempted thereby to allow the very incident which they were trying to prevent. Here, a dozen officers of both sexes and various ranks were collating, comparing and distributing information. Chief Superintendent Munro and Superintendent McHarg, with Sergeant Fellowes in attendance, were reviewing progress or the lack of it.

Nothing had been seen of Raymond Munster, but in other respects the news was satisfactory. Hanratty, scared out of his wits, had presented himself to the Tayside police and was bargaining for immunity by telling as much as he knew.

Mary Bruce had slipped up. As a natural reaction to Dora Braddle's difficulties she had transferred all their joint assets into her own name. This had left Dora unable to settle up with the legion of hard men who had been called out to watch for *Lonely Lady* and her crew. The result was that those men, when cornered by the police, had abandoned the usual rule of silence and had taken great pleasure in incriminating Dora Braddle and, with her, Mary Bruce. When Dora herself was recognised in a small Kensington hotel and taken into custody, she was understandably furious – so furious that, by the time she recovered her wits, she had already said far too much to be able to recant.

'Which is all very well,' Munro said. 'Strathclyde will have a field day. We have a wealth of information and even evidence to back it. But we do not have Munster and we still do not know his target.'

The Inspector responsible for the hour-by-hour collation of intelligence produced a sheet of telex. 'Another report here you should see,' he said. 'A burst of automatic gunfire was heard yesterday evening on Montreathmont Moor, between Arbroath and Brechin. They thought that it might be another military exercise, but the local units deny any such possibility.'

'If that was a test firing of the weapon,' McHarg said, 'he's still in the Dundee area.'

'As of last night,' Munro said. 'Yes. He could be anywhere by now. You now accept that there is a weapon and a planned assassination?'

'I have to assume it.'

'Very good of you. But even if you're right and he's still in the Dundee area, does that suggest that his target will be nearby?'

McHarg frowned. For lack of a better victim he directed

his frown at Sergeant Fellowes. 'Not necessarily,' he said at last. 'If he has a safe lodging there he may be biding his time. Dundee seems to be the only place not expecting a visit from some bigwig.'

'It is within striking distance of Aberdeen,' Munro said. 'And Grampian police are expecting an influx of politicians and oil industry executives for the Offshore Conference.'

'That's more than two months off.'

Ian Fellowes caught Munro's eye and raised his eyebrows.

'Yes, Sergeant?' Munro said.

'I've been trying to put myself in his shoes,' Ian said. 'If Mr McHarg's right, we can't do much more than warn Tayside to sharpen their watch for him and hope that every other force is taking our warnings very seriously. But suppose he has a few days in hand and his target is elsewhere. I asked myself why he'd be hanging around Dundee where attention is already focused on him.'

'Ask a silly question,' McHarg said. 'And what kind of a silly answer did you give yourself?'

There was a sneer in the Superintendent's voice and Ian Fellowes flushed. 'Let's suppose that the target is really big,' he said. 'Big enough for a successful hit to provoke the kind of speculation that followed the assassination of John F. Kennedy. Every detail surrounding that killing has been reviewed, rehashed, chewed over and discussed in the media. Books have been written about it, after endless research. With that sort of stink to follow, he couldn't afford to leave behind any loose ends at all.'

'The girl's studio is being watched,' McHarg said.

'He'd expect that. But he'll be wondering whether there was a leak. He grabbed an unexpected witness who, he must realise, was only there by chance. Will he believe that the rescuer who suddenly materialised was a passing stranger who just happened to notice the snatch and acted immediately and ruthlessly?'

'It seems unlikely,' Munro said.

'I'm wondering,' Ian said, 'if he isn't trying to find out if there was a leak and, if so, where from. If he knew that much, he could assess the seriousness of the leak before he made up his mind whether or not to go ahead.'

'And of course there was a leak,' said Munro. 'From Ailmer's workshop. But surely Dora Braddle would have told him as much.'

'Not necessarily, sir. She may have had the talkative Robert Hall killed and decided to say nothing about it rather than queer the deal. Is Bruce Ailmer, the gunsmith, under arrest?'

'Not yet,' said McHarg. He paused. When he spoke again, it was with an effort. 'You're right, Sergeant. Ailmer should be watched, just in case.'

Paul Cardinal, whose researches into his family tree seemed to have come to a dead end, was becoming a regular visitor. Keith was working at home on the routine servicing of a pair of Best English guns, listening with part of his mind while Paul, at ease in the visitor's chair, kept him company.

'I caught Superintendent Munro before he left for Edinburgh,' Paul said. 'That guy gives out information like a sparrow laying an ostrich egg, but Deborah's beau was a mite more communicative. They've picked up a whole lot of small fry for being in on the hunt for him and the Blayne lady – is she still here by the way?'

'Still here,' Keith said. 'She seems to get on well with Deborah, which is a relief. The two of them have their heads down together at the moment. But she avoids Ian Fellowes as if he had the plague although as far as I know he's FFI.'

'FFI?'

'Free From Infection. Military jargon.'

'Is that so? Anyway, apart from that, they don't seem to be doing so good.'

As if in response to the mention of her name, Deborah put her head in at the door. 'Dad, where's the *Dictionary of the Scots Language Ancient and Modern*?'

'My study, top shelf, left-hand end.'

'Thanks.' She vanished again.

'I was saying,' Paul resumed, 'that they've picked up some tough characters, none of whom knows more than that a man named Cameron, known as Grotty and believed to be an associate of Dora Braddle, promised a reward for news of *Lonely Lady*. Not one of them admits that he was willing to kill, but from their records there's little or no doubt of it. Grotty's still on the loose.'

Keith, who was using a feather to brush oil onto a striker, grunted.

'Dora Braddle was traced as far as London and pulled in,' Paul said. 'She's dropped her old pal Mary Bruce right into the mire, and herself along with her. But there's no trace at all of my old pal Raymond Munster. I suggested one or two possible lines of enquiry – that gunmaker in Dundee could do with watching – but I don't know if he'll follow them up.'

Keith grunted again.

Paul rose and prowled around the racks of antique guns. He paused at the over-decorated German wheel-lock. 'Would it be something like this that my ancestor waylaid the Russian envoy for?' he asked.

Keith raised his eyebrows in surprise that anybody could mistake the wheel-lock for a Doune pistol. 'Nothing like that at all,' he said. He put down the lockwork and wiped his hands on a paper towel. 'That reminds me. I bumped into our local librarian. To be more accurate, he came looking for me – he wants a new handle for his spinning reel. He's a fanatic about Borders genealogy. He says the Ailwand of Aikhowe, at the time your ancestor copped it, wasn't known for scattering bastards

124

around and all his sons are traceable. He thinks your Laird's Tam Elliot may be descended from a well-known reiver, the Little Jock Elliot who nearly did for the Earl of Bothwell – the lover and later the husband of Mary, Queen of Scots.'

Paul came back to his chair. 'When was this?' he said.

'Middle of the sixteenth century. As I remember the story,' Keith said, 'Bothwell was Lieutenant of the Marches in Scotland. He was making an expedition to clean up Liddesdale – one of the hotbeds of the reivers – and he'd locked up a few of the Elliots before meeting up with Little Jock Elliot of the Park. Bothwell shot Elliot off his horse but was daft enough to dismount and approach him. Elliot must have been hard hit – he's believed to have died of his wounds. All the same, he jumped Bothwell and stabbed him three times so that Bothwell had to be carried back to his castle at Hermitage.'

'They came tough in those days,' Paul said.

'None tougher.' Keith had resumed work and spoke absently. 'Those were rough times. I've sometimes thought that if the movie capital of the world had been here instead of in Hollywood, we'd have been getting Borders films instead of Westerns. After all, your Wild West only lasted for about twenty years until the railroads killed off the big cattle-drives, while the Borders had a three-hundred-year history of wars and rustling, conniving and treachery, murder, blackmail, corruption, feuds and some quite incredible feats of daring.'

Keith could have murmured on along the same lines indefinitely and Paul would have been content to listen to him. But Deborah returned, accompanied by Sheila Blayne. Their two faces spoke of barely suppressed triumph.

'I think we've cracked it,' Deborah said, waving a pad of writing paper. 'The message is quite short and it's spelled out backwards from the end – the rest seems to be mere camouflage. Sheila spotted it first. Allowing

125

for missing letters, dialect words and spelling which would have earned him a D minus in Miss Simpson's class, it reads something like this. "The arms lie buried beneath the hearth in Abbotsdale Castle. May they bring you better fortune than they have brought to me. Don't let poor Katherine starve." It's sad, isn't it?' Deborah said, blinking.

Keith held out his hand. 'Let me see,' he said.

'Where is this Abbotsdale Castle?' Sheila asked.

'Miles and miles from anywhere, up on the moors,' Deborah said. 'It's a ruin. It was ruined long before Laird's Tam went near it.'

Keith looked up from the notes. 'After what's been called the "Rebellion of the Bankrupt Earls", another Earl – Sussex – headed a punitive expedition. He burned more than three hundred towns and villages and destroyed about fifty castles and peels. Abbotsdale was among them.'

'I see what you mean about rough days,' Paul said.

Keith looked at the note-pad again. 'This could be right,' he said. 'I suppose "chimla-stane" means "hearth" in this context?'

'If he was referring to the coping stone,' Deborah said, 'nothing could exactly be buried under it.'

'We could always go and look,' Sheila said.

'And so we will,' Paul Cardinal said. 'Mr Munro asked me to be available for a few days, but I guess that time's about up.'

'The police haven't been able to find a trace of Robert Hall,' Keith said. 'Either he's dead or he's done a bunk. For his sake, I hope that he's hiding out somewhere sunny, but I doubt it. I'm interviewing a possible replacement tomorrow. But the next day's Sunday. Would that suit?'

'Surely,' Paul said. 'Shall we take my car?'

'You wouldn't get it within several miles of Abbotsdale,' Keith said. 'I'll borrow a Land Rover. It won't be comfortable but it'll get there.'

126

'It's a date. And now,' Paul said, 'I guess I'll go and see your librarian friend.'

'Don't hope for too much,' Keith told him. 'The same names cropped up over and over again, so pinning down individuals is next to impossible. To make it more difficult, a whole lot of Elliots were shipped off to Ireland when the Borders were pacified and many of them sneaked back under other names. And there was very often doubt as to who fathered any particular child.'

'It's getting that way again in the States,' Paul said.

Sergeant Fellowes and his Chief Superintendent were about to leave for home when a telex arrived. The Inspector who was acting as collator brought it to McHarg and laid it solemnly before him.

The Superintendent scanned it quickly. 'Christ!' he said.

Munro, who had been reared with all the religious superstition of the West Highlander, drew in his breath but decided that the time was not ripe for a lecture on the relationship between the Ten Commandments and the law. 'What is it?' he asked. 'Not an assassination?'

'Not quite.' McHarg glanced over the page again. 'Here, read it for yourself.'

Munro grabbed the paper, scanned it quickly and then raised his voice so that the other officers in the now hushed room could hear. 'Tayside sent an officer to observe Ailmer's workshop. The place seemed to be locked up and deserted, but Ailmer's car was nearby. The man looked round the back, found an unlocked window and took it on himself to enter. He found Ailmer unconscious, badly beaten up. Ailmer has been hospitalised. Condition stable but he may not be fit to talk for hours or even days.'

'That means—' Ian Fellowes began.

'There's more,' Munro said. 'We've been lucky. One of the neighbours, a docker who'd had a packing case dropped on his foot, was sitting at his window with nothing to do but watch the street. He identified the last visitor to the workshop from a copy of Miss Blayne's sketch. What's more, the visitor drove off in a grey Escort with a Mitchell's Car Hire sticker on it. We now have the registration number from Mitchell's. The car was hired four days ago, cash, for a fortnight, in the name of Armstrong. They're watching Mitchells, of course, but the chance that he'll return it in person is microscopic.

'We must circulate all forces,' Munro finished. 'But what do we tell them?'

'Observe, identify, arrest,' said McHarg.

'You accept that there's an intending assassin on the loose?'

Detective Superintendent McHarg had still not given up hope that events might prove him correct after all. 'It seems probable,' he said.

'It seems certain. I wish I was as sure of our course of action,' Munro said slowly. 'If the man is arrested when he does not have the weapon with him, and if he keeps his mouth shut – as he surely would – we might get a conviction on the evidence of Miss Blayne and the Sergeant here, but we might not. Even so, it would only be a firearms offence and an attempted kidnapping and we would still not know who was the intended target. Whoever hired him might still have time to send someone else, somebody unknown to us.'

'Observe, follow and report?' McHarg suggested.

'May I say something?' the Sergeant asked.

'Go ahead,' said Munro. 'But be brief.'

Ian Fellowes took a few seconds to order his thoughts. 'We have to assume that Ailmer told him that Robert Hall walked out of his job suddenly. There may be more circumstances than we know of, to confirm that he was the source of the leak.'

'But that leak has already been dealt with,' McHarg said.

128

'He may not know that. We don't even know it for sure. The body still hasn't been identified positively.' Ian left it there, but there was a faint stir of amusement in the room. The identity of the dead man remained uncertain largely because Superintendent McHarg had refused to have the body shown to Keith Calder.

McHarg looked like thunder.

'What are you leading up to?' Munro asked.

'Just this,' the Sergeant said. 'Munster would wonder where a gunsmith would go who had just walked out of his job. He only has to glance through the papers for last week to see that Keith Calder was advertising for a gunsmith. And Miss Blayne, the key witness, is staying with the Calders just now.'

McHarg's scowl was not fading. 'That's a hell of a long shot,' he said.

'I disagree,' said Munro. 'If he went to the trouble of beating the information out of Ailmer, he'd surely take the next logical step.'

'If he traced the leak to Ailmer's workshop, he'd know that his mission was uncompromised,' McHarg said. 'Neither Ailmer nor any of his staff would have known who the target was.'

'Munster may be on his way to Newton Lauder now,' Ian Fellowes said. 'I think that Keith – Mr Calder – should be warned.'

'No,' McHarg said, so loudly that the big room seemed to ring with it. He lowered his voice. 'I still have the same objection to Calder knowing more than he must. His relationship with the newspapers has proved in the past to be altogether too cosy.'

'He can hold his tongue when silence is called for,' Munro said.

'And his wife? And the girl?' McHarg was watching Ian Fellowes, waiting for any sign of rebellion. 'All we need is one hint of this to the media and then every possible occasion when an assassination might be attempted will

129

be swamped with men carrying video cameras and their cases. The task of protection would become ten times more difficult.'

'There are lives at stake,' the Sergeant said softly.

'Including the assassination target. Mr McHarg has a point,' Munro told the Sergeant. 'We'll play a different game. Get on the phone to Newton Lauder—'

The Inspector loomed over them again. 'Another message,' he said. 'Tayside put a man at the approach to the Tay Bridge. He saw the Escort heading south. It's been tracked to a small hotel in north Fife. The driver has been identified as Raymond Munster. He's being kept under observation.'

'So at last we make progress,' Munro said. 'Send a reply. He's not to be alarmed but he must be kept under observation and his every movement reported to this office. And I'm to be kept informed, or in my absence Sergeant Fellowes. Day or night. Yes?'

'Yes, sir,' said the Inspector.

'And you,' McHarg said to Ian Fellowes, 'are to stay well away from the Calders. Your sex-life can go on the back burner until this is over. Got that?'

The Sergeant looked a question at Chief Superintendent Munro, who nodded reluctantly.

Eight

Throughout the Saturday, Raymond Munster never moved far from his hotel in north Fife. Ian Fellowes was anxious enough to keep in touch, through the Edinburgh intelligence room, with the Fife officers who were on the American's tail. When the word reached him that Munster had crossed the bridge to Dundee and spent an hour in the public library, he felt a hollowness in his guts. The American was unlikely to be in search of a little light reading.

He was technically off duty on the Sunday, but he had left word that he was to be called whenever the American left his hotel. The phone woke him when morning was emerging from night and the subdued dawn chorus of midsummer was singing in the garden next door. Control was calling.

'Suspect paid his bill, cash, and left the hotel. Travelling south towards the motorway and the Forth Bridge.'

And, ultimately, towards Newton Lauder.

'Is somebody waiting to pick him up when he crosses into Lothian? And have arms been issued?'

'I'll check.'

Control called again a few minutes later. 'Edinburgh confirms.'

'Did they say more than that?'

Control hesitated. 'That was the sense of their message.'

'What did they say?'

'They said to teach your granny to suck eggs.' There was laughter in the girl's voice.

Ian was reassured but he was too keyed up to sleep again. Some day, he promised himself, he would dish out a little instruction in elementary egg-sucking to whoever had sent that message. He dressed, ate and filled in the time with housework. His small flat had never been so tidy nor seemed so claustrophobic.

The phone rang and he snatched it up. 'They've picked him up at the bridge,' said Control. 'Still following. He went round Edinburgh on the ring road and he's heading south on the A Sixty-eight. There was a personal message to you. They said, "Leave it to the professionals." '

So Munster was coming. Ian made coffee and paced the floor with the mug in his hand. The American was being given rope so that he could reveal his target. He might be heading for the target area now. But if he was coming to Newton Lauder to take action against Sheila Blayne – and himself, he recalled suddenly; another damning witness – the man would have to be pulled in, whether or not his ultimate target was known. In which case, there would be no point allowing an incident to develop at all. He kept telling himself that one unarmed officer, interfering with the actions of a trained team who had worked together in the past, could do more harm than good.

He looked out of the window. The sun was well up and the sky was clear. It was going to be another fine day and he wanted to be out in it.

He sat down and told himself to relax. He might as well have tried to fly. A glance at the phone directory would have given Munster Keith's home address at Briesland House. And Deborah was there. He tried in his mind to visualise what was to come. Munster would spy out the land before approaching. Probably he would settle down in the woods, watching the house to see who emerged. From a distance, Deborah might be mistaken for Sheila Blayne.

132

With a shock he realised that, allowing for the time which the previous message would have taken to be relayed from the car via Edinburgh and Newton Lauder to himself, Munster and his shadows must be well on the way. The sting in the tail of the last message rankled. He decided to disregard the rule-book, to head for Briesland House and make sure that no arrogant nitwit waited that extra, fatal second for the sake of conclusive evidence. Leaving it to the professionals might mean giving Munster time to kill.

He was halfway to the door when the phone rang again. He hurled himself at it.

Control's voice was troubled. 'Urgent message,' she said. 'They're held up. A tanker overturned, this side of Soutra. The road's blocked but the suspect had already gone by.'

'Tell them to commandeer a car on the other side.' Ian could hear the shake in his own voice.

'There are injured. Tailbacks are forming and the emergency services may not be able to get through. They say they must stay to help.'

'Where's the Chief Superintendent?' Munro was the only person who could authorise the issue of firearms.

'He's out of touch until this afternoon.'

Ian thought frantically. 'Is anyone available with a plain car?' he asked.

'According to the roster . . . ' She paused and he heard the rustle of paper. 'Only yourself.'

'When did the accident happen?'

'The message was timed ten twenty-two.'

He looked at his watch. Nearly eleven. The men in the car had decided that the aftermath of the accident took precedence over reporting in. Ian took a deep breath. 'Get on the phone to Briesland House. Warn Keith Calder that the assassin may be headed his way.'

He held the line. After several minutes, Control came back. 'The number's engaged.'

'Any cars out that way?'

'On a Sunday? You're joking.' Staffing was always cut to the bone on a Sunday, for financial reasons.

'Keep trying that number,' Ian said. 'I'm going out there.'

He slammed down the phone, grabbed up his personal radio and ran for the door. His car was an oven after standing in the sun. The dashboard clock told him that Munster could have reached Briesland House, if that were his destination, half an hour ago.

The engine failed to start at the first attempt. He fought off an urge to get out and run. It started at the second spin. He jinked through the side-streets like a frightened hare.

The town road, usually empty on the Sabbath, was busy with churchgoers and Sunday drivers. He had to wait, drumming on the wheel, while a Land Rover rattled past. It was followed by a short string of cars. He made ready to dart through a short gap but was balked by a van coming the other way. The last car of the string went by. He nearly missed it but realised just in time that it was a grey Ford Escort with the blunt profile of Raymond Munster at the wheel.

He wanted to dash out to Briesland House to assure himself that no bloodbath had occurred, but he forced himself to let another car go by and then turned in pursuit.

His radio was making noises at him. He picked it up.

'Mrs Calder answered,' Control said. 'Mr Calder had driven off a few minutes ago with Mr Cardinal and two ladies. They plan to visit Abbotsdale Castle. I thought I shouldn't give her the message, but she's guessed that something's up. What shall I tell her?'

If Molly was at home, the two ladies were almost certainly Sheila Blayne and Deborah. The Land Rover leading the convoy had looked very like the tatty vehicle belonging to Keith's brother-in-law. He decided that

Munster must have arrived in time to see them leave and was now following.

'Tell her from me that everything's under control,' Ian said. He hoped to hell that he knew what he was talking about.

At the junction with the main road, the Land Rover turned south. Ian watched from behind a Mercedes pulling a horse-box. Most of the other cars had stopped in the town and the Escort had dropped back. But, despite the blockage to the north, there was a steady trickle of traffic on the main road, of drivers who had given up the wait and were seeking an alternative route. Munster slotted himself into it, four cars behind the Land Rover. The Mercedes with its trailer had to wait. A placid grey horse studied Ian impassively over the tailgate as he fumed behind. The Mercedes moved at last and Ian started to carve his way through the traffic until he had the grey Escort in his sights again. The Escort seemed content to follow, a quarter of a mile behind the Land Rover. That made sense. Munster would have a better chance of attack and escape out on the moors. Ian had only a vague recollection of where Abbotsdale Castle was, but from a childhood visit he remembered that it was a desolate spot.

His car was not fitted with a police radio. He used his handset to report his position.

'The officers from Edinburgh expect to be clear in another ten minutes,' Control told him. Her voice was already becoming faint. 'They'll come after you.'

'Tell them to hurry. He could turn off at any time.'

'Noted. And there's a message from Edinburgh. The body has now been identified as that of a David MacNair, missing since Tuesday. No connection with Robert Hall.'

The traffic rolled on, chrome and glass winking in the bright sun. Sometimes he could make out the Land Rover far ahead, but he concentrated on watching the Escort from three cars behind while turning over in his

135

mind the meaning of the message. If Robert Hall was alive, where was he?

Ten miles further on, he tried his radio again. Control was unintelligible. He waited until the road climbed and tried again. Control answered, very faintly. ' . . . coming now,' said the girl's voice. 'About twenty minutes behind you.'

'How do I recognise them?' he asked.

'Three men in a blue Vauxhall . . . ' The radio went dead. Ian said a very rude word. ' . . . heard that . . . ' Control's voice said indignantly. Her voice faded for the last time. Ian tried other channels, but the Border hills were around them and the radio remained silent.

In another few miles, when the hills to be seen ahead were in England, the Escort turned right and stopped in the mouth of a road which led across the moors in the general direction of Carlisle. The Land Rover was out of sight; presumably it had made the turn and Munster was idling to let it get ahead.

Ian drove past, keeping his eyes ahead and leaning back so that his face was in shadow. He turned in another road-end and came back. The Escort had gone. His first impulse was to race after it, but he parked where the grey car had been and tried his radio again, watching the main road for a blue Vauxhall and switching from channel to channel in the hope of raising the Vauxhall and its armed occupants.

Abbotsdale Castle was somewhere among the moors ahead, but it was doubtful whether the ruins were sign-posted. If the other cars turned off, he might not find them again in time. A five-minute delay meant at least ten before he could hope to catch up. He set off, driving fast but still managing the radio with one hand. Once he heard a few words in a Northumbrian accent but, before he could ask for a message to be relayed, contact was lost again.

The road was narrow but mostly straight, rising and

dipping between the rolling moors. Miles fled by beneath him, so many miles that he was sure that the others must have turned off. Then he came over a crest to see a small grey car crawling along the road, half a mile ahead. He slowed to the other car's speed, breathing more easily.

The Escort vanished from sight. When Ian came to the same place, the road ahead was empty for a mile; then, only a few hundred yards ahead, he saw the Escort. Once again it had turned off and stopped, this time a hundred yards into a rough track across the moors. A trace of dust hanging in the air suggested that the Land Rover had passed that way.

Ian had no option but to drive on, past the grey car and the silhouette of Raymond Munster. He watched in his mirror. The grey car moved off along the track. When it was out of sight, he turned in the road and went back.

The track was rough. It had never been planned but followed an ancient route where horsemen had found it easiest to pass, avoiding rocky terrain and sudden patches of peat-bog. Heather had re-established itself along the central hump between wheel-ruts, so that he could hear it dragging against his sump. The Land Rover would be making better time here than either of the following cars.

The landscape was becoming more broken. The track, which had been made by horses and since little used except by the occasional naturalist, archaeologist or hiker in search of history, was so irregular that even the Land Rover had had to make small detours.

Raymond Munster, in the Escort, decided that the car had come far enough. There would be no profit in doing what he had come to do unless his retreat was secure. He wondered for a moment whether the occupants of the Land Rover had chosen this method of shaking him off and were now descending to another road by some other track, but he decided to ignore that risk.

He had been careful and they had no reason to expect a follower.

On the seat beside him was the shell of a large tape-recorder. He had spent much of the previous day in his hotel room, transferring the modified rifle out of the camcorder case, which had been much too clearly represented in the girl's sketch. But there was no need for such refinement at the moment. It took only a minute or two to demount the gun from the case and pocket the weight of the spare magazines. He now had a small submachine-gun in his hands and more than enough ammunition for his purpose. At close range, it would be devastating.

Fifty yards ahead, the track crested a saddle between two low hills. He left the Escort in the middle of the way and walked forward until his view opened up. Ahead, the track wound its way to another hill which rose sharply out of flat bogland. A ruin topped the hill. Most of the walls were tumbled, but from fragments of battlement and the corner of a tower it seemed to have been a small castle. The Land Rover stood below the hill and small figures could be seen climbing towards the ruin.

There would be no chance of approaching the ruin unobserved. Very well, let them come to him.

Near the car was the remains of a sheiling, a rough cottage built by a shepherd or drover as a summer shelter. Being of no importance, it had not been razed by Sussex's troops and most of the dry-stone walls stood at least waist-high. Even the Land Rover could not pass his car where it was. It made a perfect site for an ambush.

Luck, he decided, was now making amends for the ill chance that had brought the artist to Broughty Ferry and a rescuer close behind. Reassured by the gunsmith, who had certainly been too terrified to lie, he had decided that his mission could go ahead. But, having a day or two in hand, he had nevertheless also decided to visit Newton Lauder. If the man Calder, who had advertised for a gunsmith, had taken on Bruce Ailmer's decamping employee, it might be interesting to see what other involvement Calder might have.

He had barely settled into a hiding place in the woodland overlooking Briesland House when the Land Rover went by and he had recognised the woman. With a sudden jolt, he had also recognised Paul Cardinal – a much more interesting target. Two for the price of one, he told himself. It only needed the third, the red-haired man who had assaulted his wedding tackle, to make his day.

The third enemy had nearly blundered within sight of Raymond Munster, but caution and instinct had combined to save him. Ian's car was out of sight beyond an earlier hump in the track and from behind a haphazard rocky outcrop he watched Munster settle down to wait. Above and far beyond the sheiling, he could see the ruins on their small hill.

He tried his radio again. It was no more than a useless plastic box tarted up to look as though it had a hi-tech function.

If he went back to try to establish contact with the officers in the blue Vauxhall, God alone knew how long it might take or what might happen in the meantime. Munster's view forward was cut off by a swell of the ground. It might take him an hour to work his way through dead ground to where he could break cover and run for the castle, but an hour might be enough . . . and if it was not, would the outcome be any the worse? With luck, he should at least be in time to intercept the Land Rover on its way back.

Fumbling in his haste, he hunted until he found paper and a pencil. He scribbled a hasty warning of an ambush ahead, stuck it under a windscreen wiper and set off at a determined jog-trot, trying simultaneously to watch for sudden bog-patches and to keep an eye open in Munster's direction to ensure that there was always a hill, or at least a fold of ground, between them. As he jogged he sweated and the midges came out of the damp ground and dined royally on him. He slapped at them and damned his luck and the midges and the warm sun, but most of all the danger to Deborah. And the others, he reminded himself.

Keith's party arrived, panting gently, at the level of the castle. Much of the stonework had been blown or tumbled outward so that the small hill was peppered with masonry blocks, almost lost in rank grass and heather. Between them they were carrying two spades, a crowbar and a sledge-hammer, but there were other tools waiting in the Land Rover.

Sheila looked around the barren countryside and shivered. 'What a desolate place!' she said.

'It was never meant to be welcoming,' Deborah said. 'Just impregnable.'

'And it was already a ruin when Laird's Tam visited here, more'n two hundred years ago?' Paul said. 'If I got you right, it had already been a ruin for a hundred years. We don't have anything that old in the States. The fights this old place must have seen!' He moved through the remains of a doorway into what had been the base of the tower. There was a deep recess in the remains of the corner wall. 'Would this have been the fireplace?'

The others had followed him. Keith took a quick look and shook his head. 'The loo,' he said. Paul looked blank. 'The john,' Keith explained. 'Just a shaft coming down with a slab at each floor level. The more senior you were, the higher you lived. Those below had to look out for themselves. Which suggests that the private apartments were over here. We'll try the far side.'

He picked his way carefully to the other end of the tower. The walls were lower. A drift of fallen stones gave him a start and he pulled himself to a seated position above head-level. 'Here we are. There's the remains of a flue in this wall.' He turned to look behind him, almost losing his balance. 'I thought so. Most of the wall went

140

outward into the courtyard – it must have done, if the hearth was exposed when Laird's Tam visited. There's been another fall since, or else he pulled some more wall down to cover his hidey-hole. We've got some stone-heaving to do.'

They set to work. Deborah and Sheila tossed the smaller stones away while Keith and Paul, aided by occasional use of the crowbar, rolled the larger masonry aside. The top of the fireplace opening emerged but, as they progressed, the heaps of discarded stones became more intrusive and the work more laborious. It was another half-hour before they came down to a solid slab of stone and traces of ash from a long-dead fire.

'Looks as though it's been here for ever,' Paul said doubtfully.

'It's been here a long time,' Keith admitted. 'Of course, there may have been another fireplace. Or Deborah's reconstruction of the message was speculative. We may have got some of it wrong. Or Aikhowe may have beaten us to it. But I'm damned if I'm giving up just yet.'

'Me neither,' Paul said.

Keith seated himself on a large stone block. 'Take a rest while one of the girls goes back to the Land Rover for the jack.'

When they resumed work, they managed to get first the crowbar and then the jack under a corner of the heavy slab. At last it came upright. They jumped away as it toppled back against the tumbled masonry.

Underneath was sand. Keith ran his fingers through it. 'Bone dry,' he said. 'Thank the Lord!' He wiped his forehead with a moist handkerchief, leaving a trail of dirt.

'You two men sit and rest,' Sheila said. 'You've worked hard. We can do this bit.'

Paul and Keith were happy to cool off while the two girls scraped the loose sand aside with their hands. Keith went down to the Land Rover for beer.

Deborah stopped work suddenly. 'He wouldn't have buried a dead sheep here, would he? There was something about a widow's ewe in the letter.'

'Fish it out,' Keith said. 'They'll have sewn it into a sheepskin so that the tallow would protect it. That's what they wanted the widow's sheep for.'

Deborah placed a bundle in his hands. 'So Aikhowe never found the message in the Bible.'

'There's something else,' Sheila said. 'Wooden. A round box.'

'The top of a small keg of powder,' Keith said.

'I believe you're right.'

Paul cut the stitches. The sheepskin had hardened but they broke it apart. Inside, three objects were wrapped separately in more sheepskin.

When the last wrappings were forced open, Paul sat back. 'One flintlock pistol,' he said disgustedly. 'I thought they went in pairs. And two fancy sword-hilts. Why only the hilts and not the whole sword?'

'Go on digging,' Keith told the girls. 'But you won't find sword-blades. The Scots didn't make good blades. They were imported from Soligen by the bundle. But the Czar would probably have ordered good Damascus blades from Spain.'

'But I don't understand,' Paul said. 'Surely a Czar wouldn't order just one pistol and send his envoy all this way for it. He'd've ordered at least one pair, probably more.'

Deborah was digging with the crowbar. 'Blame your ancestor,' she said. 'If he had a trod after him – a posse – for a fortnight, he and his pals would have wanted to be armed with the best quality pistols they could lay hands on. If there's anything else here, I can't find it,' she said.

'That makes sense,' Paul said. 'I wish it didn't.'

'There's somebody coming,' Sheila said.

Keith dropped his discarded jacket over the 'arms'.

A figure stumbled through one of the openings. 'It's Ian,' Deborah cried. 'Ian, what's happened to you?' She hurried towards him, scrambling over the tumbled stones, but stopped suddenly as she realised the state he was in. He had been into a bog over his knees and sweated through the rest of his clothes and he was panting as though he had never breathed before. Blinded by the sweat in his eyes he had stumbled over a rock and skinned his hands and knees.

Keith helped him to find a seat. 'Tell us whenever you're ready,' he said.

Ian breathed deeply for a full minute and then, between deep gasps of air, told them in brief the story of their followers and of the ambush. 'I don't think he can see here from there,' he finished, 'but he might have moved and I couldn't chance it. I had to come a long way round.'

Sheila began to shake. 'He's come for me,' she said. 'God! That woman wasn't with him?'

'Stay cool,' Ian said. 'Dora's being held and the man's a good mile off. We won't let him get you.'

'Of course not,' Deborah said.

Paul held out his hand. 'Give me your radio,' he said. 'I'll climb as high as I can and see if your pals in the Vauxhall aren't in range yet.'

Ian handed over his radio. Paul scrambled up to where Keith had sat earlier and then climbed cautiously along and up the crumbling wall. He tried every channel. 'No good,' he said at last. 'Frankly, I reckon your set's on the blink. I'm not even getting an atmospheric hiss. I'm coming down.' He descended cautiously.

'We have a problem,' Keith said. 'I think we hike out cross-country and go for help, leaving the vehicles to be collected later.'

'No way,' Paul said. 'Point one, Ian's friends in the Vauxhall may be armed but with what? Pistols? If they show up and Munster hears them coming they could walk into an ambush set by a man with an automatic weapon. And, point two, for the first time we know where Munster is. Let him get out from under and there may be no stopping him. We don't know who his target is, but your country gets visited by a hell of a lot of big shots from all the countries in the world. For Christ's sake, he could trigger World War Three.'

Ian nodded.

'Well, all right,' Keith said. 'But how?'

'You don't have that pistol with you,' Paul said. It was a statement rather than a question.

'No.'

'You picked a hell of a time to stop carrying it. Okay, so we go in unarmed against an armed man. Your cops have been doing it for years.'

'We're not exactly unarmed,' Keith said. He lifted the flintlock pistol, pulled out the ramrod and inserted it into the barrel.

'That thing?'

'It's killed before. And,' Keith said, 'it's still loaded. The tallow in the sheepskin seems to have kept it nicely greased. The flint's sharp and well set. But the only ball we have for it is still up the spout.' He searched his pockets and found a paperclip with which he probed the touch-hole. 'The powder seems dry enough. Of course, I've only got one shot with it, if that, so we've got to plan with care. I wouldn't back myself to hit a man at more than about thirty yards. His cut-down Ruger won't be very accurate at that range and he's only got small-bore capability; but he's got a lot of it, and even a two-two Long Rifle bullet can kill if it finds the right place.'

'You'd better give it to me,' Paul said. 'I'm trained in pistol marksmanship under combat conditions.'

'My job,' Ian said.

Deborah shook her head dumbly.

'Have either of you ever fired a flintlock before?' Keith demanded. 'I thought not. The delay would confuse you and you wouldn't know what to do in the event of a

144

misfire. What's more, you two seem to have dressed for a picnic.' He looked with disdain at Paul's pale slacks and Ian's white shirt and bandage and then glanced down at the muted clothes which he wore out of the habit of years. Keith liked to be ready for an impromptu stalk or a seat in a pigeon-hide at any time. 'Even out of the corner of his eye, he couldn't fail to notice you. And you couldn't swap clothes with me. You're both fatter than I am.'

'Not fatter,' Ian said. 'Thicker.'

'Your word, not mine.'

'Dad, this is crazy,' Deborah said. 'You can't do it! What do you think Mum would say if she knew?'

'Consider it said. Now, would you rather that your Sergeant took it on? Or that we let somebody else be assassinated?' Deborah was silent. 'Right,' Keith said. 'We'll take our time – I want the sun in his eyes. Let's synchronise our watches. Then I want to see if that keg can produce some fine, dry powder to prime the flashpan. After that, here's what we do . . . .'

From behind a half-tumbled piece of stone wall, perhaps the remains of a former sheep-pen, Keith and the Sergeant looked out at the killing-field.

'You can make out his head above and to the right of the pale stone,' Ian whispered.

'Well done,' Keith said softly. A whisper carries further than a murmur on still air. 'You've a good eye for country. And you were right about the sun being behind him. If he turns it'll be right in his eyes. You know what to do?'

'You've told us all fourteen times. You're sure you can manage?'

'Provided you hold his attention.' Keith looked at his watch. 'We're running out of time. Get back to your car.'

Ian nodded and set off, crawling through dead ground and then jogging round behind the swell of a low hump.

His personal midges followed him and he was regretting ever leaving city streets.

A shallow stream brought Keith closer to the sheiling. Crawling was difficult, with the flintlock pistol to be kept dry and safe. The trigger-guard had been broken off at some time and he was none too sure that the half-cock position would be reliable.

The course of the stream turned where it came up against an outcrop of rock. This was probably as close as he could get for the moment. He raised his head cautiously and then held still, studying the ground. He was still sixty yards from his target, too far for a shot even if the pistol fired.

He chose the next part of his route with care. He wanted to move silently and from behind Munster, but he wanted to stay low so that the descending afternoon sun would not throw his shadow forward into the man's peripheral vision.

Then there was nothing to do but wait and hope that his nerve would hold. At first the temptation to slap at the midges was almost overpowering but, as the cold water round his ankles cooled his bloodstream, the burning of the bites died away. He could feel the sun on his back, but his feet were cold.

From nearby, a cock grouse took fright and lifted, crying 'Go-back, go-back.' Its low flight took it almost over Munster's head. Keith froze, head down, certain that the man would read the sign of another's presence as he himself would have done. But when he risked a cautious look, the man had not turned his head.

He checked the pistol again. There was another factor which he had not mentioned when discussing the plan. If the ball were locked into the barrel by corrosion, the pistol would almost certainly burst. He very much hoped that he could get close enough to Munster to bluff him. Or perhaps he could clobber him with the butt – which, it seemed, had already served that purpose at least once, two centuries earlier. Given half a chance, Keith decided, he would drive him into the peat like a nail.

His watch told him that something should be happening. He held his breath and listened. Faintly on the still air came the sound of the Land Rover. It was still a long way off. Keith peered cautiously through a chink in the wall. Too soon to come out of cover. Munster was moving, getting ready for the massacre.

The sound grew, slowly. The Land Rover would be in sight within a minute or two. Keith looked in the opposite direction. Ian's car came out of the dip and bounced along the rough track.

With his attention divided between vehicles approaching on both fronts, Munster would surely not think to look behind him. Keith rose and, feeling naked, set off over the heather. Fifty yards. Forty-five.

The Land Rover came over the crest, roaring. It held to the ruts. The driver, if any, was invisible.

Keith was running, his noise drowned. Forty yards. Thirty-five, thirty.

The Land Rover swerved off the track, climbed a boulder and rolled gently onto its roof. The stone which had been holding down its accelerator fell off. The engine slowed to a tickover and died.

Keith ran, as he thought, from heather onto grass; but it was green algae and weed covering a stagnant puddle of bog. He was slowed, splashing loudly. Ian's car was still a hundred yards off, its engine noise not yet loud enough to cover the splash. Keith was still twenty yards from the sheiling, his feet sinking. Munster half turned, saw him and began to swing the converted rifle.

Ian, from his car, saw the puff of smoke from the flashpan but there was no sound of the shot. The pistol had misfired.

Keith saw the muzzle of the automatic weapon settle on him and knew that he was dead. There was nothing for it except to go through the drill, knowing that it would take

147

a second or two. And he did not have a second, let alone two. He re-cocked the pistol and closed the flashpan. As if in a bad dream, his feet were held and every movement seemed to take an hour. Munster screwed up his eyes against the sun.

Impelled by instinct or by reasoning faster than conscious thought, Ian put his head out of the car window and raised his voice until it cracked. 'Dora!' he yelled. The sound echoed back from the hillsides.

It was Dora Braddle's reputation for infallibility that had brought Munster to her in the first place. He had lifted her money on an impulse, but on consideration he had wondered whether the move had been a wise one. Ever since, he had been expecting that formidable lady to appear, bent on revenge and restitution. He looked round for a moment.

Keith turned the pistol on its side and gave it a sharp slap in the hope of drifting a pinch of powder through the touch-hole to re-prime the flashpan. He was the focus of Munster's attention again. The small muzzle was settling on his belly. He took quick aim and pulled the trigger. The action snapped loudly.

As the first bullet grazed Keith's right ribs, the pistol fired. The ball took Munster through the upper chest. The rest of the short burst went high.

Keith struggled forward, dragging his boots out of the sodden peat. But Munster was not down. Spitting blood, he was bringing up his weapon again. Keith threw himself forward and tried to sink.

Paul Cardinal arrived, racing down the track in the wake of the Land Rover and vaulting over the stonework to smash Munster down. He picked up the converted rifle and tossed it out onto the heather.

'You okay?' he asked Keith.

Keith dragged himself to the wall, spitting peat and acid water, and climbed over. 'I think I just died,' he said. 'But I'm alive now.' He pulled up his shirt. The wound was barely a scratch. He let his shirt hang. 'He only hit me once,' he said. 'I never count the first three or four.'

Munster was lying, half propped against the stones. Blood from his mouth was streaking his chin while a stain was spreading over his shirt. They knelt down on either side of him.

'Who was your client?' Keith asked him.

Munster slowly shook his head and coughed more blood.

'He'll never tell you that,' Paul said. 'They never do. But . . . who was your target?' he asked Munster. 'Tell me that and we'll try to get you to hospital.'

Munster was struggling to speak.

Ian's head appeared above the wall of the sheiling. Then Sheila and Deborah arrived, panting, from the other direction.

'Yes, who?' Ian said.

Munster fought for breath. He made a sound like the purr of a cat. Then there was another rush of blood, his eyes rolled and he was limp.

'I think he's gone,' Paul said. 'If not, he won't tick more than a minute or two. He was trying to make a word. President, maybe?'

'Or Prime Minster?' said Keith.

Deborah had turned her back on the scene but she was calm. 'Prince somebody?' she suggested.

'Could be,' said Paul. 'Or maybe he was just asking us to promise him something. Maybe we'll never know.' He looked up. 'Here come your friends, galloping to the rescue after the danger's past.'

The blue Vauxhall was bumping along the track. Ian went to meet the other officers. 'This is how you hold the egg,' he said.

Nobody saw Paul Cardinal go; but when the first flush of excitement was over, they saw that he had gone. With him went Ian Fellowes's car and the flintlock pistol.

Nine

A week had gone by. Much of the first pandemonium had abated. With the assassin dead, police activity had been reduced to sporadic enquiries in the hope of identifying his client; a concentrated effort towards prosecuting Dora Braddle, Mary Bruce and all their cronies; and ceaseless bickering at a high level as to who had been dilatory or negligent or, alternatively, rash and impetuous in his duties.

The general attitude of the police was that Sergeant Fellowes had scored a triumph; also that Keith's shooting of Raymond Munster had been fully justified and should be supported when the matter came eventually to the inevitable Enquiry. The only dissenting voice had been that of Detective Superintendent McHarg, who had done himself no good in the process and was understood to be deep in the bad books of the ACC (Crime).

Keith and Deborah were working together, at the upstairs workbench at Briesland House, on an old but beautiful hammer-gun, the internal lockwork of which had been sadly neglected. Using porous pads which had been impregnated with a mild abrasive, they were patiently removing all traces of corrosion from the tiny parts when Molly appeared in the doorway.

'You have a visitor,' Molly said. She was smiling the special smile that usually meant a surprise. She stood aside. 'Mr Hall.'

150

Robert Hall walked diffidently into the room and stood in his habitual droop.

'But you're dead,' Keith said stupidly.

Deborah, startled into carelessness, let a mainspring slip out of the spring-vice and flip across the room.

Hall stooped to recover it. 'Not very,' he said. 'I can't use that as an excuse for letting you down. I came to apologise. And to ask if the job was still open.' Unconsciously, he picked up a pad and began to polish the spring in his fingers.

'It could be open,' Keith said. 'I took on a youngster. He starts next week, and so does the contract. But he was going to need far more supervision than I'll have time for. I could use you both. First you'd have to explain. Sit down.'

'This I've got to hear,' Molly said.

Hall gave her his shy smile. 'You have the chair, Mrs Calder,' he said. 'I'm quite used to standing at a bench.'

'So why didn't you turn up?' Keith asked.

'Were you kidnapped, Mr Hall?' Deborah put in.

Hall shook his head. His moustache drooped less as he smiled. 'Please call me Bob,' he said. 'It's what I've always answered to. No, I wasn't kidnapped. I was obeying orders.'

'Whose orders?' Keith said.

'I don't know the whole story. But I can make guesses at most of it. Have you seen today's papers?'

'Not to do more than glance at the headlines. We've been busy.'

Hall put down the now shining spring and scratched his moustache thoughtfully. 'About a month ago, you probably saw that the research laboratory of a pharmaceutical manufacturer had come up with a new drug. It won't cure anything, but it helps to restore the body's immune system and so suppresses the symptoms of AIDS, among other diseases, and prevents it progressing. This

151

morning's papers announced that J and D Pharmaceuticals of Glasgow had taken over the firm, lock, stock and barrel, in the teeth of strong competition from America and Germany.

'The man who gave me my orders called himself Smith and he wouldn't say who he was working for. But I saw his car. It isn't difficult to find out who owns a particular car if you know the registration number. The car belonged to J and D Pharmaceuticals. So while I was under orders to lie low, I thought I might as well lie low in Glasgow and do a little digging.' He shrugged. 'I can be as nosey as the next man at times.

'The chairman of J and D was in Switzerland, raising additional finance, but it was common knowledge that a takeover battle was going on. I think that he was the target. The vice-chairman was known to be dead against the deal.'

Keith remembered the last sound made by the dying Munster. 'What's the chairman's name?' he asked.

'Prescott.'

Keith and Deborah exchanged a glance. The purring sound was explained. 'How did you come into all this?' Keith asked.

'From what Smith said when he was briefing me, there really was an employee of Bruce Ailmer who found out what was happening, got scared and walked out. He talked to a pal before vanishing and the story came to the ears of somebody who connected it with J and D Pharmaceuticals.

'They couldn't trace the man and the takeover was at such a delicate stage that publicity could have upset the cart and let the Americans or the Germans in. Rather than go to the police and risk a story in the media, they decided to replace the original, now vanished, man with another gunsmith. I was unemployed, so they got onto me.'

'How?' Deborah asked keenly.

'Through the Job Centre. I was told to apply for

a job and let my prospective employer prise the story out of me. That would make sure it got to the police by a back door and the right amount of information would pass. Not too little, not too much, as the advertisements used to say. The police would be chasing the assassin. Meantime, I suppose that they were taking their own steps to keep their chairman out of harm's way.

'After I'd seen you, Mr Calder, I met Smith in Edinburgh and told him that you were going to pass the story on to the police. That's when he told me to lie low. I didn't like it. I *wanted* that job with you. But, as he said, if I went to the police they could soon prove that I was a ringer. And I needed my fee. This morning, I was paid in cash and told that I needn't hide out any more.'

Keith looked him in the eye. 'The rest of your references were your own?'

'Absolutely.' Bob Hall hesitated and nerved himself. 'Do I still get the job?'

Keith looked at Molly for advice.

Molly Calder had only one formula for such occasions. 'You'd better stay to lunch,' she said. 'And I'd better go and put it on.'

'Can I come and help you?'

'I'd like that,' she said.

Alone again, father and daughter looked at one another. 'That seems to explain the loose ends,' Deborah said at last. She picked up a lock-plate and began polishing rust off the inner surface.

'All but one,' Keith said. 'Paul Cardinal seems to have been exactly what he made himself out to be. So why did he bugger off suddenly, taking the pistol with him? Did I tell you that I had an apologetic note from him, telling me where he'd left Ian's car?'

'I know that,' Deborah said. 'Ian told me before he went off to fetch the car. I think Mr Cardinal was desperate to have that pistol. Perhaps he was afraid you'd change your mind or he'd lose the toss.'

Keith scratched his head. 'Get out those sword-hilts,' he said. Deborah put down the lock-plate and went to a cupboard below a rack of pistols. She unwrapped the two hilts and laid them carefully on the bench. Keith looked at them with affection. 'Top quality basket hilts by Walter Allan of Stirling,' he said. 'Complete with the Russian imperial crest. And in damn nearly mint condition. With that story attached to them, what sort of price would you expect them to make at auction?'

Deborah studied the hilts with her eyes half closed. Keith encouraged her to read and digest the reports of prices fetched at arms auctions. 'To a museum or a keen collector, not less than ten grand apiece. Maybe twenty.'

Keith nodded. 'You're not far off. If anything, a little on the light side. Why, in God's name, would Paul Cardinal prefer a crummy old horse-pistol with the trigger guard missing? And the butt broken, probably over somebody's head, and patched with side-plates of some sort of horn. The sort of thing we'd put in the catalogue at a hundred quid and be glad to accept thirty.'

Deborah blushed scarlet. 'I'm afraid that was my fault,' she said. 'He got me aside and asked me how you'd recognise a Doune pistol.'

Keith began to understand. He spluttered with laughter. 'And you said that it would have a ramshorn butt and no trigger-guard?'

'Yes.'

'And he didn't realise that ramshorn was a shape, not a material.' Keith wiped his eyes. 'Oh well! All he was really after was to have a pistol on the wall and be able to say that it had belonged to one of his ancestors. I dare say he'll be just as happy with what he's got. But, you silly juggins, the period was too early for the ramshorn shape. The Czar's pistols would have had fishtail butts.'

154

Father and daughter worked on while arguing amicably over when the first ramshorn butts had appeared on Scottish pistols.

'Dad,' Deborah said suddenly, 'would there be anything in one of your books to tell us who was the Big Bug at Carlisle Castle when Laird's Tam was taken there?'

'Now there's a thought,' Keith said.

Sheila Blayne returned to Dundee. Somehow her work never again quite attained the miracle of that drawing of the Tay, but the confidence it had given her stood her in good stead and she is building a useful career illustrating children's books.

Her studio flat now doubles as a salon for the younger students. As a single parent she could be seen to be as free a spirit as themselves and the barriers came down.

Even when she found that she was pregnant, Sheila's new confidence was unshaken. She considered carefully and decided that she could get by without dropping a bombshell into the life of one whom she still considered godlike. After all, he had certainly saved her life as well as presenting her with another life to cherish.

The possession of a sandy-haired son with blue eyes and a square jaw is enough. She is happy.

Author's Note

The historical element in this story is not to be taken too
seriously. But in trying to avoid taking too many liberties
with the facts, I was greatly aided by George MacDonald
Fraser's book *The Steel Bonnets*.

G.H.